The Stall

The Stall

Susan Ulrich Kruse

Copyright © 2024 Susan Ulrich Kruse

All rights reserved.

ISBN: 9798335324052

Acknowledgements

Thank you to my sister-in-law, Kathleen Miclot. You were the first person to hear this crazy story. Your encouragement inspired me to think it was good enough to tell the world.

A big thank you to Mari Husman and all my other proofreaders. You ensured the voices in my head would make sense to the world.

Many thanks to my friend, Logan Taylor Webb, for my cover photography. Your talent is a gift to the world.

And the biggest thank you of all to my husband and sons, Tim, Zack and Ian, for their encouragement along the way. You are my world.

Chapter 1 - December 10, 2023

Holiday plans had always been a bone of contention for Collin and Lauren. It wasn't that Lauren disliked visiting Collin's family, but it was that he outright refused to see hers. Hoping for a smoother conversation, and perhaps a change of heart for Collin, Lauren suggested they go out and discuss Christmas plans over drinks.

"Mom said she'd like to know our decision soon," Collin said, picking up his beer and swirling it around. "Sound ok if..."

"When did we start coming here?" Lauren asked, interrupting him mid-sentence.

"What?"

"When did we start coming to George's?" Lauren repeated, adding the name of their favorite local bar. In her mind, George's hadn't been open for more than a year but the tables, chairs and floor bore so many marks of abuse that it was possible they'd been around for quite a while now.

"Two years ago, right after we met," Collin reminded her.

That's right, she thought, and nodded her head.

She'd moved into her apartment right after arriving in Chelsea in 2017. A relatively quick decision, but a good one. Summit held too many painful memories and her new neighborhood was *just* far enough from there.

"Anyway, I was saying I think we should plan to drive up to my folks' this year. Ben, Angela and the kids will be there, too."

Lauren knew Collin loved his family dearly and that they were really important to him. But past experience had taught her that Christmases at Collin's parents' home in White Plains typically included a round or two of arguments, usually between him and his brother, Ben, over the weaknesses of the other's favorite NFL team. She'd escape to their backyard with a bottle of wine and listen for them to eventually make up, their laughter signaling it was safe to come back inside and rejoin the group.

Visiting her side of the family entailed nothing more than a trip to see her brother, Parker, his wife, Steph, and their two girls in Summit, New Jersey – but Collin could barely keep those interactions civil. Once she accepted that neither Parker nor Collin had any intention of getting along for her sake, holidays were never split equally again.

As if he could read her thoughts, Collin asked, "You're not seriously suggesting we go see Parker?"

Lauren was silent.

"When are you going to accept that I'm not spending my holidays in his house ever again? *You* can go but I won't waste my vacation time on a man who doesn't respect me – no, outright judges me – and you too, by the way."

"I know you think he and Steph are judgmental..."

Collin cut Lauren off before she could finish.

The Stall

"Yes, they are. They saw your move to Chelsea as escaping, not as independence. In their minds, you're wasting your talents making coffee for strangers and they certainly don't understand why you don't want to move back closer to home."

Collin paused, sighed, and then added, "Even though he won't say it, Lauren, I know Parker blames me for keeping you away."

She knew he had a point. Parker had been pretty harsh when she announced that she had found an apartment in the city, accusing her of running away when their family needed to *"be there for each other."* Although she had already turned 20 at the time, and it was her decision to make, Parker didn't agree and his over-protectiveness came across as harsh criticism.

It had been 11 years since her parents were killed in a car accident in 2012. At the time, Lauren was 15 and Parker was 20. Up until then, their family had been living a very comfortable lifestyle in a beautiful neighborhood in Summit, New Jersey, a township popular with executives for its green, dense trees, nice restaurants and good schools. The "Garden State" indeed. Except it was one of those trees that ended her parents' lives - a curve taken too fast driving home from dinner late at night.

Their parents' trust put Lauren under the immediate guardianship of Parker and he did his best to be mother, father and brother, all at the same time. He made sure she finished high school and enrolled her in a local arts college – supporting Lauren's natural eye for photography. But even with the best of intentions and his devoted support, it was, of course, impossible to fill the emotional void left by their parents. Especially their mom.

Mrs. Brown had been everyone's cheerleader and confidante, the type of mother you could talk to after a bad day, and the first person you'd want to tell on a good one. She and Lauren's father made a great team and Lauren admired how her mother supported her husband's career, attending frequent work dinners and charity events. There were many nights when Lauren would watch her mom get ready for an evening out, helping her choose the perfect outfit and shoes. Her mother *loved* shoes.

Fortunately for Lauren and Parker, their parents' sizeable net worth ensured that neither of them would have to worry about finances for the rest of their lives. And at the age of 18, while engrossed in her photography program and making friends easily, Lauren received her substantial inheritance. That's when the fun *really* began. It wasn't long before she found her social life more interesting than the classes. Eventually, the all-night parties turned into day-drinking and her love of photography nearly evaporated with the hangovers. Almost to the day of her 20th birthday, she dropped out and drove to Chelsea.

Sensing Collin had made up his mind about Christmas, Lauren decided to get up.

"Can you grab the waitress and order me another pinot noir, please."

Collin nodded but didn't smile. Lauren sensed he was tallying up her previous glasses in his head as she headed toward the bathroom.

The ladies' room was empty as Lauren walked in and headed to the second stall. Unbuckling her jeans and turning around, she sat down and let out a sigh, thinking about her life since moving to Chelsea. She had an amazing apartment, a nice job at Starbucks, Collin, and not much else to worry about. The fact that Parker didn't like Collin, or approve of how sh e spent her time, hardly crossed her mind – except when it came to making Christmas plans. Then it always came up.

A few moments later, the door to the ladies' room opened and Lauren heard the click of high heels coming towards the stalls. She chuckled to herself.

Heels? Not really George's vibe, but ok.

Looking down at her own feet, Lauren grimaced at the wet floor and heard a 'shlep' sound as she moved her foot and repositioned it into a somewhat drier spot.

"Gross," she said quietly to herself. "I hope that's beer down there."

She never saw the door coming.

Stars. Lights. An incredibly sharp pain drilled itself into the top of Lauren's head.

"What the fuck?" she yelled out.

"Oh my God! I am so sorry!" a woman's voice called out. "The stall door wasn't latched. I thought it was empty."

"Well, it's NOT! Shit!" Lauren struggled to keep from slipping off the toilet, and quickly put out her hand and caught herself on the wall. Just as she opened her eyes, she heard the ladies' room door open and the heeled woman walked out.

As Lauren sat on the toilet, tears streamed down her face and she wondered if her head was bleeding. Balling up some toilet paper, she blotted her hair gingerly, fully expecting to see blood. None.

"Oh man," was all she said as she slowly stood and opened the unlatched door. "Shit. I guess I didn't lock it."

Sniffling, she wiped her eyes and wondered if her mascara had turned her into a raccoon for the rest of the night. She didn't have to wait long to find out.

Her face, in fact, didn't look like she'd been crying at all. But that wasn't what Lauren noticed. She noticed, well, *everything else*. From head to toe, Lauren looked amazing. Her jeans and sweatshirt were gone, replaced by the most stunning red dress she'd ever seen. And on her feet, black Christian Louboutins.

Heels. Just like Mom's.

"I must be dreaming. I must have been knocked out," she mumbled. She shook her head and blinked hard. The red dress and heels were still there.

And with an, "I'm getting out of here," she abruptly opened the bathroom door and stepped back into the bar.

Except. It. Wasn't. What lay in front of her was a beautifully appointed, bustling restaurant with tables full of well-dressed couples, laughing, toasting, and talking.

"What?" she whispered under her breath and immediately stopped dead in her tracks.

No one seemed to notice the beautiful woman in the red dress and heels. No one, except for a man sitting alone at a table in the middle of the room. When he finally caught her eye, he gave her a quizzical look and mouthed a single word.

"What?"

Then he smiled and tilted his head to the side as if to say, "Come on."

Chapter 2 – The Table

Lauren stood still, frozen, trying to breathe and unsure of what to do next. Finally, as if in a trance, she slowly started walking toward the stranger at the table. He rose and pulled out her chair.

"Here you are, gorgeous," he said as she slid slowly into her seat. "I just requested the dessert menu."

As he sat back down, he looked at her and said, "So, I was saying we should think about moving over to Brooklyn. New neighborhood, new faces, and get away from everything you've dealt with."

Lauren watched him talk, not really comprehending what he was saying except for the comment, "...get away from everything..."

What am I getting away from? What have I dealt with? she wondered.

"And we really should think about our July 4th plans. It's a Thursday this year. When we spoke about it before, you mentioned going to see Parker and his clan. I think that would be great. What do you think about..." he stopped abruptly.

Lauren's eyes were huge pools of confusion.

What? July? she thought to herself. *It's only December 10th.*

Concerned, the man leaned in and whispered, "Lauren. What's wrong? What happened?"

Lauren didn't reply but blinked quickly at him as if signaling confusion and fear.

"Lauren," he repeated more forcefully, this time loud enough for those at the neighboring tables to turn and stare. Still, Lauren did not reply.

"Did something happen in the bathroom?"

And with that, Lauren spoke. "No, um, not really. I'm not sure."

An outright lie, but what could she say?

Yes, I just got smacked in the head and now I'm sitting with a complete stranger and I have no idea where I am.

"Ok. We're heading home. You need to rest."

In what seemed like seconds, the man called for the check and handed his valet ticket to the maître d. As he signed the bill, Lauren glanced down and read the name of the restaurant printed at the top: The Highmark. She'd never heard of it. Then she saw his signature. Theo Briggs.

Theo. Theo.

A completely unknown name.

Theo didn't say much to her on the way home, silently maneuvering his black Audi S8 through the city streets. Lauren's mind was not silent, however. Thoughts were racing through her head.

What am I doing? How do I snap out of this?

Lauren was jarred back to reality when Theo pulled up in front of an apartment building.

"I'm going to take you up and then I'll park."

The Stall

And with that, Theo stepped out and came around to open Lauren's door. As Lauren stepped out of the car, she noticed the doorman, smartly dressed and all smiles, open the front door of the apartment building.

"Good evening, Mr. Briggs. Ms. Brown."

Lauren had to force a smile. The doorman obviously knew them.

Do I live here?

Theo nodded at him as they entered the building, his hand on Lauren's elbow.

"I'll be back down in a moment. Lauren doesn't feel well."

As the elevator dinged open, Lauren was relieved that Theo pushed the button and selected their floor: Twenty-seven.

A few moments later, Lauren walked into Theo's apartment. The surroundings were beautiful. Simple, understated elegance. A modern cook's kitchen on the right and straight ahead a living room with floor-to-ceiling windows. Lauren looked down the hallway to the left and saw what appeared to be a bedroom and bathroom.

Oh. She thought to herself. *Yeah, bedroom. One. Ours.*

Lauren knew she had to clear the fog from her head.

"I'm going to take a shower," she said to Theo, who was still holding onto her elbow.

"Are you sure? Do you want me to come in and help you? Make sure you don't fall?"

"No, I'll be ok, I promise."

"Ok, I'm going to park the car and then I'll be back up."

"Ok, thanks. Sorry about how tonight ended. I just don't feel well."

Just get through this, Lauren told herself. *This has got to end soon.*

Lauren waited until Theo had left the apartment before she moved an inch. As soon as the door shut, she grabbed her phone from her purse, hit the 'Phone' app and looked for the first name in her Favorites: Collin.

"What the...?" she whispered. His name was not there. "That's not possible."

Hitting the keypad, she dialed his number from memory and nervously waited for him to pick up. After four or five rings, an elderly woman's voice finally answered.

"Hello?"

"Hello. Is this Collin's phone?"

"Collin? No, there's no Collin here," the woman replied.

Lauren stood in shocked silence for a moment, then spoke.

"I'm...I'm sorry, my friend used to have this number."

"Oh, I see. Yes, I got this phone in January. Maybe he had the number before me. I've heard those phone companies reuse numbers sometimes."

"Ok...well, thank you," was all Lauren could manage to say as she hung up. She could feel her sense of confusion escalating towards panic.

Looking around, she knew she had to orient herself to Theo's place, and fast. A quick look through the kitchen. No problems there. Walking down the hall to the bedroom, she quickly found a large, custom closet, pulled the doors open, and gasped. Chanel, Prada, and more designer labels than Lauren had ever seen, hung in front of her eyes. Pulling out some drawers, she found various pieces of lingerie and smiled for just a moment, running her fingers over the fine silk material. A few drawers

The Stall

down, she found what she was looking for – a long sleeve, long pant pajama set.

Perfect. Safe.

Within minutes, Lauren leaned back against the marble wall of the shower, letting the hot water do its best to wash away whatever was happening. But Lauren feared it wouldn't help.

I'm just biding my time. But what next?

And with that thought, she slid down the wall until she sat with her knees up to her chest. And back came the tears.

Twenty minutes passed before Lauren felt she had enough courage to get off the shower floor. Dried off and in the pajamas, Lauren silently walked toward the living room, unsure how the next few moments with Theo would turn out. With a sigh of relief, Lauren found Theo in a chair, fast asleep.

"Thank God," Lauren said under her breath and turned around to go to bed.

Perhaps it was the hot water doing its job, but Lauren had a very brief, hopeful thought as she sank into bed.

Maybe this is all a dream.

And with that, she looked at her phone. The date shone brightly on the home screen.

10:33pm

Sunday, June 2, 2024

Exhaustion pushed her over the edge into sleep before her brain had a chance to register what she had seen on her phone.

Chapter 3 - The Dress

The bright sunshine finally woke Lauren. With her eyes still shut, she stretched out her arms and legs, smiled to herself and thought about how deeply she had slept. Finally opening her eyes, the view of the ceiling broke her smile.

This isn't my room.

She struggled to remember where she was and how she'd gotten there. But then she did.

The stall door. Theo. Shower. Bed.

She anxiously glanced over at the other side of the bed. No Theo.

That's good. Now I've got to get out of here and figure out what the hell's going on.

Reaching over to the bedside table, Lauren picked up her phone and stared at the home screen.

11:05am

Saturday, June 1, 2024

That's strange, I thought yesterday was Sunday. I must have been delirious last night.

Walking out to the kitchen, Lauren smiled as she picked up a carafe of coffee sitting on the island and found it full and warm to the touch.

"Well, this is a good start," she told herself and she opened the refrigerator to see if there was any creamer around. Again, another surprise, as she found not only her favorite brand but the refrigerator was stocked full with all her favorite foods.

"Well, Lauren, I guess you live here," she said to herself.

Next to the carafe, Lauren found a note. "Hope you feel better. Going to the gym and then to see if Grandma needs anything in her new place. See you mid-afternoon. Love you, Theo."

Giving herself a short, determined speech, Lauren poured her coffee and walked toward the bedroom.

Ok, time to get to work.

Within 30 minutes, she had showered and chosen a casual outfit from the closet which fit amazingly well.

Guess I shouldn't be surprised, especially if I bought this.

Locating her purse exactly where she left it last night, Lauren looked inside for the keys to her car and apartment. Gone. Nothing but a keycard. Then it dawned on her.

Of course. I don't live at my apartment anymore. The keycard looks like what Theo used last night. But do I still drive?

Lauren shook her head in frustration but then was immediately glad she had given her elderly neighbor an extra apartment key for emergencies.

Hopefully Mrs. Adams will be home.

The Stall

Minutes later, Lauren exited the elevator and walked toward daylight.

"Good afternoon, Ms. Brown. Lovely day we're having!" The doorman greeted her as she walked through the front door.

"Good morning. So sorry to be a pain, but could you please hail me a cab?"

"No problem. Happy to help," he cheerfully replied. "And you've got the number to call if you need a ride back home?"

"Um, you know, I don't think I saved it in my contacts. Could you give it to me again, please?"

"Of course, Ms. Brown."

As Lauren took the card from his outstretched hand, she noted the phone number and the name of the apartment building printed in beautiful gold script.

"Thank you so much."

Within moments, she was in the back of the cab.

"Chelsea. 21st and 9th please," she directed as the driver pulled away from the building.

Lauren closed her eyes, summoning up the courage to face whatever lay at the end of this ride.

"Here you are."

Looking toward her building, Lauren smiled at the sight of her familiar life.

"How much?" she asked the driver.

"Nothing. It's charged to the apartment."

Lauren raised her eyebrows at the idea, but didn't argue.

"Ok. Thank you," she replied and exited the cab.

Ok, brave girl, let's go home.

Inside the building's foyer, she walked over to the intercom and scanned the button labels for #2A. It read, "Campbell".

No, that's MY apartment.

Then her pulse started to race as reality sank in.

I don't live here anymore...Find Mrs. Adams!

She finds #2B. "Clark."

Oh no. No! No!

Mrs. Adams was not there.

Suddenly, a man came down the staircase, about to walk past her and toward the door.

"Excuse me, I'm looking for..." and then she stopped.

Am I supposed to say my apartment? He'll think I'm crazy. Well, maybe I am.

"Mrs. Adams. She lives in 2B."

"Oh, the older lady. She moved out. Sorry."

And with that, he walked out.

With no one else to ask, and certainly no way to get into her apartment, Lauren walked slowly out the building and called the number on the card. Dejected, she rode back home in a cab - although she wasn't quite sure how to define 'home' anymore.

Walking back into Theo's apartment, she noticed for the first time a large number of photos around the living room. Pictures of smiling faces. Faces that looked like Theo's.

The Stall

Must be his parents.

But none of the faces were familiar.

"Who *are* you people?" she wondered aloud.

For the next hour, Lauren walked around the apartment, opening drawers and closets.

Clues. There must be clues to who Theo is or how I ended up with him.

But none surfaced. Even a desk that appeared to be Theo's was relatively empty except for some mail and a laptop - shut and locked. Frustrated, she headed to the kitchen.

If I live here, there's got to be wine.

And within minutes, she had settled down at the island with a glass. Her favorite vineyard, of course.

It was almost 3:30pm when the apartment door opened and Theo called out.

"Hello? Lauren, you home?"

"In here," she answered from the kitchen.

"Hey, how was your day? Did you work?"

Crap! I have a job.

Lauren tried to mask her panic.

"Uh, no, no I was off today. Just rested mainly."

"That's great, but hey, I'm glad you're here because there's no way I could wait any longer for this!"

And with that, Theo turned and went back into the hallway.

"Shut your eyes!!" he yelled from the doorway.

"Oh, ok," Lauren replied.

She could hear Theo walking back toward her.

"Hold out your hands."

Lauren did as he asked and immediately felt a box being laid in her arms.

"Ok! Open!"

Lauren opened her eyes and looked down to see a large white box tied with a red ribbon.

"Surprise!! I saw you eyeing this when we were out shopping last week and so I knew I had to get it to cheer you up!"

Theo was almost giddy as he stood in front of her.

"Well, go on! Open it!"

"Wow, ok, well, thanks," Lauren smiled at his boyish enthusiasm and wondered what could be in the box.

Let's see what this is.

Turning around, she laid the large box on the island and slowly untied the ribbon. With a few tugs, the lid came off.

"What is this?" she asked as she looked down at tissue paper tucked across the top, completely covering the contents. Theo didn't say a word. He just stood there smiling.

Lauren unfolded the paper and then gasped. Inside the box was a dress. A beautiful red dress. The dress she'd worn last night.

"Do you love it, honey?" Theo beamed. "You're going to look amazing in this!"

Lauren managed a small smile and replied, "Um, yes, it's, it's...gorgeous. Um...thank you."

"I'm so excited," Theo gushed, totally oblivious to her distress. "I can't wait to see you in this! But that's only half the surprise!"

The Stall

He moved toward Lauren and wrapped his arms around her waist, pulling her close.

"I was able to get reservations at that brand new place in Midtown we heard about. Tomorrow is their soft opening and we're going! I'd love for you to wear this."

"Ok, sure, sounds perfect," Lauren smiled weakly. "But sorry, what's the name of the place?"

"The Highmark."

And with that, Lauren felt her legs go weak. The room began to spin and everything went dark.

Chapter 4 - Work

The hum of the city coming to life eventually woke Lauren. There was no stretching this time, no sleepy start to the day. Instead, Lauren looked over and saw Theo laying there. She let out a deep sigh and turned over toward the bedside table, reaching for her phone.

6:05am

Friday, May 31, 2024

She bolted up straight in bed, almost waking Theo as he stirred next to her. It was at that moment that she realized she wasn't exhausted. Or delirious. Yesterday *was* Saturday. Time was going backwards. In an instant, her stomach lurched and she barely made it to the bathroom in time.

Lauren had no idea how long she sat on the bathroom floor but eventually felt well enough to stumble back to bed. The room was still spinning when she passed out.

The Stall

It was almost 9:00am when Lauren awoke again. Out in the kitchen, she found a note next to the carafe of hot coffee: "Didn't want to wake you. I've gone to work. Call me later. Love you."

"How am I supposed to call you when I don't know your number?" Lauren said out loud. Then added, "Oh duh, I'm sure you're in my phone."

Yes - his name, work and cell number were in there. In her Favorites. Where Collin used to be. Lauren hit the work number and it began to ring.

A friendly, female voice answered. "Good morning, Anderson, Thomas and Cooper. How may I direct your call?"

"Um, hi. This is Lauren calling for Theo Briggs," Lauren made a mental note of the company.

So many names, maybe it's a law firm.

"Oh, hello, Lauren. It's a pleasure to speak with you. Yes, Theo is in. One moment please and I'll connect you."

Within a few seconds, Theo picked up, "Hello, darling. How are you?"

"I'm fine. Is everything ok? Your note said to call."

"Oh yes, you just looked a little pale this morning when I left. Wanted to make sure you were feeling ok."

Lauren laughed to herself.

Yeah, I puked my guts out in the bathroom. Oh, and time is now going backwards for me. But other than that, I'm fine, thanks.

"I'm fine."

"Good, do you work today?"

This time Lauren was prepared. She quickly pulled up the app on her phone and saw that yes, she worked today.

"Yes, at noon. Gotta go."

And with that, Lauren hung up - just as Theo said, "Ok, love y..."

After a quick shower, Lauren headed out of the apartment. Google confirmed that her Starbucks café wasn't far from Theo's apartment. She decided to walk.

Walking in, Lauren was immediately relieved that she actually knew *this* place. Everything was exactly as she remembered it and everyone greeted her with the usual, "Hello" and "Hi ya." Completely normal. And when she saw her best friend, Abbie, was working the same shift, she was almost giddy.

The afternoon went well and Lauren felt grateful for the routine. The familiar work and faces made her feel grounded. She felt so good, in fact, she made plans with Abbie to go out after their shift ended.

Just before they headed out, she texted Theo.

Lauren: *Going out with Abbie. They got a new puppy. I'll be home for dinner.*

Abbie and Lauren decided to walk to a bar just around the corner from the cafe.

"I got this," Lauren offered as she ordered wine for herself and a beer for Abbie. As soon as they sank into the booth, Lauren reached for the wine in front of her and took a long drink.

Ok, brave girl, let's go.

"This is nice," she said to Abbie.

"Yeah. Cheers!" Abbie replied as they clinked their glasses together.

"So, listen, there's something I need to ask you."

Lauren took a deep breath and looked Abbie straight in the eyes.

The Stall

"Has anything strange been happening to you, like over the past 2 to 3 days?"

"No, not really. Normal bs with Jack. And we're still arguing about who gets up to let Ginger out to pee in the middle of the night. He says I should do it because I don't have to get up early. Stupid reason." Abbie smiled, winked at Lauren and took a long drink of beer. "Why do you ask?"

"Um, well, nothing. Forget about it," but Lauren had already started to tear up. "I'm sorry. I haven't felt like myself for a while."

"Oh, honey," Abbie reached for Lauren's hand. "I'm not surprised, with everything you've dealt with this year. I'm sure it's just the prolonged mental stress from all that. It takes its toll."

Lauren stared at Abbie.

There it is again. People keep referring to everything I've dealt with. WHAT HAVE I DEALT WITH?

"You're right. I probably need more sleep, less screen time," Lauren said and tried to fake a smile.

Over the next 20 minutes, Lauren sat quietly as Abbie talked more about their new puppy, her plans for the summer, and asked Lauren's opinion on a new hairstyle. It was finally too much for Lauren.

"Hey, I should probably get going. Theo will be home soon."

Abbie smiled with her eyes and nodded in agreement as she finished her beer.

Once outside, they gave each other a big hug and then headed in opposite directions. After a second, Abbie hollered back at Lauren, "Hope you feel better. We'll talk more tomorrow!"

Lauren turned and waved goodbye. Heading towards home, Lauren thought to herself, *no, actually we won't.*

The smell of something wonderful greeted Lauren as she walked into the apartment. Theo was in the kitchen, paying very close attention to something simmering on the stove.

"Hello, beautiful!" his voice rang out as he heard the apartment door close.

"Hi."

"How's Abbie? Oh, and how's their puppy?!" Theo asked, wiping his hands on a towel and picking up two glasses of wine.

"Thanks!" Lauren replied as she accepted the glass. "She's good. Puppy is good. Goes pee a lot."

"I've heard they do that," Theo laughed and motioned toward the seats at the kitchen island. "Sit. We're ready to eat. Lobster ravioli & garlic knots coming right up!"

"It smells amazing!" Lauren replied as she sat down. The rumble in her stomach reminded her she hadn't eaten much, or kept much of what she'd managed to eat, in her stomach.

Over the ravioli, bread and wine, Lauren got Theo talking, carefully peppering him with questions about his day. By the end, she learned she was right – he was a lawyer. A junior partner, in fact, at Anderson, Thomas and Cooper and worked in mergers and acquisitions. His best friend, Cam, had just proposed to a woman named Kelly. They wanted to get together and have a little engagement celebration sometime soon. Theo and Cam had known each other since undergrad at Penn. Cam worked as a defense attorney in the city. Lots of nasty clients, lots of press. Got a lot of them off. But since Theo seemed to adore his friend, Lauren withheld judgement.

What's Cam short for? she wondered. *Cameron maybe?*

Lauren had also learned that Theo was very close to his mom and grandmother, although he hadn't said their names yet. Mom and grandma lived in the city somewhere. No mention of a dad.

By the time they'd finished dinner, both Lauren's stomach and her brain were completely full. Lauren let out a small yawn but quickly tried to cover her mouth.

"Oh, sorry," she said as she smiled and then put her hand on her stomach. "I'm so full. This was amazing."

Theo smiled.

"You're very welcome. I'm glad you enjoyed it."

Then he scooted his seat closer.

With her mind racing, Lauren fought the initial urge to lean back.

If I'm going to find out what happened to Collin and how I got here, I've got to keep this up.

And with that thought still in her mind, Theo leaned over and kissed her softly on the lips.

"Theo, would it be ok if we call it a night? Food coma is setting in fast."

Lauren let out a yawn - fake this time.

Theo took the hint and slowly leaned back in his seat.

"Sure, honey. Tomorrow's the weekend. Let's sleep in."

She smiled.

"Sounds great."

And in her mind, she added, *actually Theo, tomorrow is going to be Thursday and I'm finding out what the hell happened to Collin.*

Chapter 5 – The Investigation

It only took an instant for Lauren to grab her phone as soon as the alarm went off. Holding it to her chest, she played a little mental game.

Maybe if I squeeze my eyes shut really tightly, I won't see what I think I'm going to see.

But as she slowly opened her eyes, she stared at what she had predicted.

7:35am
Thursday, May 30, 2024

Of course.

That was her initial silent reaction. But it was soon followed by something that actually surprised her: Fear.

What happen to Collin?

Walking out to the kitchen, Lauren found the carafe of hot coffee waiting for her. A strange feeling of appreciation for Theo rose up, but she quickly tucked the feeling away. She knew what she needed to do today and she booted up her computer at the kitchen island.

Lauren's hands shook as she typed in the Google search: Collin James Hunt, DOB August 2, 1997.

Lauren paused and took a deep breath.

Am I ready for this? Here we go.

She hit Enter.

Numerous results quickly filled the screen.

CHELSEA MAN FOUND STABBED

MANHUNT UNDERWAY FOR ALLEY KILLER

POLICE LEADS DRY UP FOR DECEMBER KILLER

"DEAD? OH MY GOD!" Lauren yelled out into the empty apartment. Lauren's eyes burned with instant tears.

Lauren spent the next hour alternating between staring at her computer screen, reading article after article, and collapsing into a sobbing mess on the cold kitchen island. It was almost 11:00am when she came out of her heartbroken fog, exhausted, numb and all cried out.

She couldn't believe what she'd learned. Collin was found stabbed to death in an alley in Chelsea in the early morning hours of December 11th. No witnesses. No one charged. His funeral was held Monday, December 18th in his hometown. Attended by family and friends.

Questions flooded Lauren's mind.

Where was I on December 11th? Was I at the funeral? Of course, I would have been there.

And then suddenly a lightning bolt hit her.

The Stall

Oh my God! December 10th was the night we were at George's! He was killed after we left!

She could feel her mind shift into overdrive with seismic force.

I'm going to find out who did this.

Suddenly her phone pinged - a reminder notification from her Starbuck's app that she had a shift in one hour. A quick text exchange with Abbie solved that problem. She'd cover it. Abbie wasn't scheduled to work and luckily, she'd be home from the pet rescue center by then. She and Jack were getting a puppy. Lauren tried to act surprised when, of course, she already knew about the dog.

Back at her computer desk, Lauren quickly worked out a plan:

Call Collin's parents
Call Collin's brother and wife
Find a reporter from one of the newspaper articles that will talk
Find a police report

Making the list proved to be the easy part. She updated the list as the afternoon progressed.

Call Collin's parents - *left voicemail 1:15pm*
Call Collin's brother and wife - *left voicemail for Ben 1:17. Left voicemail for Angela 1:20.*

She didn't have to wait long for a response.

At 1:25pm, Angela texted her. Lauren quickly read the message.

Angela: I know you contacted Collin's parents and Ben. How DARE you! We have NOTHING to say to you. Don't EVER reach out to any of us again.

Wait, what?

Lauren re-read it - her mouth open in shock. But that shock quickly changed to anger.

WTF? Yeah, we'll see about that. Should I reply? Probably not the best idea right now.

"I'd better get out of here," she said out loud and headed downstairs for a walk to clear her head.

The doorman greeted her with his usual smile.

"Good afternoon, Ms. Brown. Heading out? Would you like me to call a cab for you?"

"No thanks, just a walk today. If Theo comes home before me, please let him know I'll be back before dinner."

And with that, Lauren headed down the street, planning what she'd say the next day when she would visit Collin's parents.

Chapter 6 – The Parents

By 8:00am, the doorman had called Lauren a cab and she was on her way to White Plains.

Earlier that morning, she'd hardly batted an eye when she glanced at her phone:

7:15am

Wednesday, May 29, 2024

She'd given herself a little pep talk as she grabbed her coffee and left the apartment.

Let's go, brave girl.

Now, as she rode along the familiar route to Collin's parents' home, possible scenarios of what was to come played out in her head.

Would Collin's mother be upset to see her? Would she even open the door? What would his parents say to her?

Still wrestling with those unanswered questions, Lauren arrived shortly before 9:00am.

As the car came to a stop, she said to the driver, "I'm not really sure how long I'm staying."

"It's ok, I'll keep the meter running. Mr. Briggs is paying for this anyway."

Lauren smiled and then stepped out.

I'm not sure he would if he knew the reason.

It took two rounds of knocking before Lauren heard a woman's voice call out, "I'm coming!"

Moments later, Collin's mother, Barbara, opened the door and immediately stared wide-eyed at her unexpected guest.

Lauren spoke first.

"Hello, Barbara."

Barbara's face filled with distress and with a trembling hand, covered her mouth.

"Lauren...," Barbara choked as tears filled her eyes. "I'm sorry, I can't talk to you. Please leave...now."

"Wait!" Lauren sputtered as the door shut in her face.

"I just want to speak with you!" Lauren pleaded loudly. "Please! I want to talk about what happened to Collin. Please!"

A few moments later, Collin's father opened the door.

"Lauren, please, we asked you not to contact us. You need to leave now. You have to go or I'll call the police. I'm sorry."

His eyes implored her to understand.

"I know, I'm so sorry for surprising you like this. I just need to know more about what happened to Collin."

The Stall

"What happened?" his face reddened. "You already know! He's gone! You want to know more? Maybe you should have been with him that night and then you'd know!"

Once again, the door slammed in Lauren's face.

Lauren stood at the door for the next few minutes, shaking and unable to move from the shock of what had just happened. She could hear both parents weeping from inside the house.

Do they really blame me for what happened? Was I supposed to be there with Collin? But I WAS! I WAS at George's!

Eventually, Lauren slowly walked back to the cab and spent the next hour riding home in numb silence.

About 45 minutes after arriving back at the apartment, her cell phone rang. It was Theo. The niceties were gone from his voice. No, "Hello, darling."

"Did you go see Collin's parents today?"

"What? I mean, yes, I did...but how do you know?"

"I get car charges emailed to me immediately, Lauren. I know Collin was from White Plains. It wasn't too much of a stretch to figure out. You *know* you shouldn't contact his family. You need to let that go."

Lauren mentally kicked herself for not being more careful.

Of course, Theo would see the bill. I should have taken a city taxi.

She needed to get off the phone before she made more mistakes.

"I know, I'm sorry," she tried to appease him. "I just wanted to talk to them."

"Well, you can't!" Theo practically shouted into the phone and then paused and took a deep breath. "Listen, I have to go but we will talk more about this tonight." And with that, Theo hung up.

It may have been the shock of Collin's parents' reactions to seeing her, having the door literally shut in her face twice, or the realization that her trip only added questions to her list rather than answer them – but Lauren had drunk two generous glasses of wine by the time Theo got home.

He didn't say a word when he found her in the kitchen, but gave the half empty wine bottle a questioning look before he turned and silently went back to the bedroom to change clothes. It was ten minutes before he came back out.

"Do you want to talk about this before or after we eat?" Theo asked as he opened the refrigerator door.

"I'm so sorry, Theo," Lauren apologized. "I don't know what came over me. I guess I'm still kinda dealing with everything."

From the softening look on his face, she could tell he bought it.

"I'm sorry I barked at you on the phone. I was just completely caught off guard. I had no idea you'd ever go up there."

He walked over to where she was sitting and gave her a long hug. With that, a silent truce was called.

The rest of the night was spent sharing dinner, watching tv, and finishing the open bottle of wine. Maybe it was the wine. Maybe she was still stung by the rejection of Collin's parents. Or maybe she just needed something else to think about. For whatever reason, when they went to bed, Lauren didn't try to avoid Theo's advances. For just that moment,

The Stall

Lauren pushed the thought of Collin out of her mind and forgot Theo was a stranger she'd only met a few days ago. Lauren fell asleep quickly that night with Theo's arm draped over her in what felt like familiar comfort.

Chapter 7 – The Reporter

The alarm woke Lauren at 7:00am and her phone confirmed what she already knew.

Tuesday, May 28, 2024

Lauren reviewed her plan and crossed out the first two.
I can forget about those.

~~Call Collin's parents – *left vmail 1:15pm*~~

~~Call Collin's brother and wife – *left vmail for Ben 1:17. Left vmail for Angela 1:20.*~~

Find a reporter from one of the newspaper articles that will talk

Find a police report

Lauren slowly typed in the same Google search that she'd used a few days earlier: Collin James Hunt, DOB August 2, 1997. Her eyes scanned the search results until she settled on:

The Stall

POLICE LEADS DRY UP FOR DECEMBER KILLER

She remembered this article. It was the most recent of all the ones she'd found and the reporter had stuck to mostly facts instead of the more sensational details she'd read in the others. She quickly scanned the article for the reporter's name – Sandra Kennedy – and her email address. Lauren typed out a message before she could change her mind.

Hello Ms. Kennedy, my name is Lauren Brown. My boyfriend was Collin Hunt. You wrote about his murder last December. Could we meet sometime soon? I live in Chelsea but can meet anywhere that is convenient for you. Thank you.

Within 30 minutes, Lauren saw a reply.

Hi, I can meet at 6:00pm today. Don't know a location yet but I'll find something and let you know. I am tall with brown hair and wearing a yellow shirt. Sandra.

At 5:45pm, Lauren received an email with the name of a café not far from the apartment. She shot a quick text to Theo about picking up a shift for Abbie and then was out the door within 60 seconds. Walking into the café, she looked around nervously, somewhat hoping the woman wouldn't show up.

Am I really ready for all my questions to be answered?

But Sandra was already there. Lauren waved to the reporter and walked towards her.

How exactly does one start this conversation?

"Hi. Thanks for meeting me," Lauren said as she and Sandra shook hands. Then Lauren added, "I know this must be a bit strange."

"Not really, I actually get a lot of strange requests in my business. But I am curious about why you reached out to me."

"Yeah. Actually, I was hoping you could tell me everything you uncovered while reporting on Collin's story."

Lauren sat back in her seat and waited.

"Hmmm," Sandra paused and looked at her curiously. "Ok, sure. But why. And why now?"

Lauren knew she had to tread carefully.

"A lot happened in December. A lot. I think my brain has blocked a lot of memories for me," Lauren sighed, mostly for effect. "I'd like you to help by telling me everything."

That's as much as I'm going to say.

Sandra bought it.

"Ok. Basically, he was found unresponsive in an alley not far from George's Bar & Grill. He'd been stabbed twice in the stomach."

Lauren immediately felt her own stomach start to ache and she squeezed her eyes shut as they began to tear up. Sandra noticed Lauren's painful reaction.

"Are you ok?"

"Yes, please go on."

"Ok. CC cameras from the jewelry store next door showed him leaving Geoge's at 2:00am, which was closing time, and stumbling past the store, headed south."

Lauren's ears perked up.

South?! We lived north of George's. He was going in the wrong direction!

The Stall

"South?"

"Yes. Police received a call from someone who spotted Collin slumped over just inside the alley one block away. He was pronounced dead by emergency responders who arrived at the scene."

Lauren must have appeared to be in shock, as Sandra reached out and took her hand.

"I'm very sorry, Lauren. Did I answer all your questions?"

Lauren nodded, tears falling down her cheeks.

Just as Sandra got up to leave, Lauren asked, "Oh. What did the police say about me?"

Sandra gave her a strange look.

"About you? Well, the employees who'd been at George's that night told police that Collin and his girlfriend, which everyone identified as you, were at George's together. They said you'd had some drinks but they weren't sure if you two had an argument or you just wanted to go home. Either way, you left shortly after midnight. Collin stayed. No one said much else."

Lauren couldn't respond. There was nothing to say. Sandra turned and left.

Lauren sat in silence at the cafe for the next few hours, waving off the waitresses who would stop by to ask if she wanted anything, asking if she was ok or needed help.

I left him. I left him behind and someone killed him.

That was all she told herself, over and over and over.

By the time Lauren walked into the apartment that night, Theo had gone to bed. She quickly showered and then crawled in, replaying the conversation with Sandra in her head.

We were there. I left. He left. He went the wrong way. He was found at... What time did she say?

Suddenly she realized she had forgotten to ask some very critical questions.

How much time passed from when the cameras picked up Collin leaving George's to when the police were called? And who else was seen on the footage?

Lauren was excited to speak with Sandra again and decided it would be fine to call her in the morning and ask some follow up questions over the phone. But then Lauren stopped.

Actually, in the morning it won't really be a follow up. It'll be the first time she's spoken to me.

In some strange way that made Lauren feel better.

Chapter 8 - The Re-Do

Lauren wasn't sure which was louder - her alarm going off at 7:00am or Theo groaning his displeasure.

Monday, May 27, 2024

"What are you doing? It's a holiday," he moaned into his pillow.

Holiday? Oh shit. Memorial Day. He's off work.

"Oh, I'm so sorry, I should have turned the volume down. But I, um, picked up another shift from Abbie. Not super long. Gotta go. I'll text you later and we can make plans."

Lauren snuck into the kitchen and typed out a quick email to Sandra.

Hello Sandra, my name is Lauren Brown. My boyfriend was Collin Hunt. You wrote about his murder last December. Could we meet this morning? I know it's a holiday but I'm off work today and really need to talk with you. I live in Chelsea but can meet anywhere convenient. Thanks.

Within 20 minutes, Lauren saw a reply.

Hi, I can meet at 9am today. Don't know a location yet but I'll find something and let you know. I am tall with brown hair and have a blue shirt on. Sandra.

Yellow one day, blue the next, Lauren chuckled to herself.

At 8:45am, Lauren received another email with the name of the café – the same place as before. Within minutes, Lauren was shaking Sandra's hand – again.

"Hi. Thanks for meeting me. I know this must be a bit strange."

"No, I get a lot of strange requests in my business."

Does she use that line on everyone?

"Yeah. I was hoping you could tell me everything you remember about Collin's story."

Sandra looked at her curiously. Lauren knew what was coming next.

"Sure, but you've heard all this before. Why talk about it now?"

"A lot happened in December and my brain has blocked a lot of memories for me," Lauren sighed, again, mostly for effect. "It would be a huge help if you can tell me everything."

Again, Sandra bought it.

"Hmmm. Well. Basically, he was found unresponsive in an alley not far from George's Bar & Grill. He'd been stabbed twice in the stomach. Security cameras from a jewelry store next door showed him leaving George's at 2:00am, which was closing time, and stumbling down the road headed south. Police received a call from someone who spotted Collin slumped over just inside the alley one block away. He was pronounced dead by emergency responders who arrived at the scene."

Lauren nodded, processing the news again and preparing to ask more questions.

"What did the police say about me?"

Sandra paused and then answered, "The employees at George's that night told police that Collin and his girlfriend, which everyone identified as you, were at George's together. You left shortly after midnight. Said you were really intoxicated and Collin got you a cab home. Collin stayed."

Intoxicated. Oh. That's new. So... I left him... Oh my God. No wonder his parents blame me!

Lauren sat in stunned silence. After a moment, she was ready with more questions.

"So, the cameras showed him leave at 2:00am?"

"Yes, that's right."

"What time was he found?"

"I think the police received a call around 2:30am."

"So, about 30 minutes later."

"Yes, about 30 minutes."

"Ok, was anyone else seen on the security footage?"

"George's is a pretty popular place, so yes, there were a lot of others leaving the bar."

Lauren's face must have lit up because Sandra looked at her strangely.

"You seem happy about this news."

Be careful.

"No, of course, not. What else can you tell me?"

"The police checked out everyone seen on camera and also put out a call for anyone in the vicinity of George's at or after 2:00am. They questioned everyone but nothing ever came from it."

Be very careful, Lauren.

"Ok, thanks a lot. I truly appreciate you going through this with me."

Sandra got up and smiled. Just before turning to leave, she said, "You're welcome. But of course, you heard all this last December. I'm sorry I wasn't able to give you anything new."

Lauren stood, shook her hand and said goodbye. Sitting back down, she was overcome with conflicting emotions. On one hand, she had learned that her drinking had led to the decision for her to leave, which in turn had led to Collin's death. But she was also hopeful.

There's security footage out there with faces on it - and one of them may have been the person who murdered Collin! On Friday, I'm going to find it.

Lauren headed back home.

Walking in, she found Theo making plans.

"Great, you're back! We're meeting Cam and Kelly in the park in an hour."

Lauren smiled and nodded, adding, "Fun! I'll go change clothes."

This is my new normal. Put on a good show, brave girl.

Chapter 9 – The Detective

Lauren spent the weekend thinking about the best way to get the camera footage. By the morning of Friday, May 24, she was ready.

Would the jewelry store have it?

A quick call to the store confirmed the police had taken the recording and never brought it back.

Ok, so that's progress. But does one just walk into the police station and ask to speak to someone? Probably not. Better to call.

With a deep breath, Lauren pulled up the Google search results about Collin's death and found the precinct that handled the investigation. Within minutes, she was calling their non-emergency number.

"Hello, my name is Lauren Brown and my boyfriend, Collin Hunt, was murdered last December. I would like to speak to the detective who investigated his death, please."

"Just a moment."

A few moments passed.

"Detective Harding. How can I help you?"

"Detective, my name is Lauren Brown and my boyfriend, Collin Hunt, was killed last December after leaving George's. Do you remember the case?"

"Yes, Ms. Brown. I remember it and I remember speaking with you."

Oh, yes, of course he would. I've got to be careful here.

"Yes, thank you. Um, I'd like to find out what happened to the security footage from the jewelry store next door. I'd like to see it."

"The footage should be in our evidence room. But may I ask why you want to see it? I watched it multiple times and you know we interviewed everyone we could reach. Why do you want to see it now?"

Lauren paused.

"I appreciate everything you did in December, Detective Harding. I really do. But I want to see it to help me..." Lauren paused again, "process some grief I'm still dealing with."

There, play the sympathy card.

Lauren held her breath.

Detective Harding exhaled, "Ok, come by the precinct tomorrow at 9:00am and ask for me. I'll find the video and have it ready for you."

Lauren bit her lip.

I can't do it tomorrow. Tomorrow has already happened.

"Well, Detective, I hate to say this but today is the only day I have off work this week and I'd really like to put my mind at ease. Could we possibly arrange for me to see it later today?"

Lauren held her breath again.

"I see. The later the better. Would 4:30pm work?"

"Yes, thank you so much. I really appreciate this, Detective. I'll see you at 4:30pm."

Lauren arrived at the station at 4:15pm and waited for Detective Harding. A few minutes later, he walked into the lobby and waved at her.

Act like you remember him.

"Hello Detective. Thank you so much for helping me with this today."

"Sure, it's nice to see you. How have you been?"

Lauren silently laughed.

Oh, if only you knew.

"I'm doing ok, thanks."

Keep it short and sweet.

Lauren followed Detective Harding back to a small, brightly lit room where she found a table and two chairs. On the table was a laptop.

"Normally we'd watch this footage at my desk but I thought you might like some privacy."

Lauren smiled and sat down in the chair. Detective Harding sat next to her.

"Ok, I cued this up to start at 1:45am on December 11th. I'll hit play and you'll see some people come out of the bar over the next few minutes. I'll pause the video each time someone comes out so you can see their faces."

Lauren nodded quietly and looked at the laptop's screen as Detective Harding hit Enter to start the video.

1:45:00am - 1:45:25 No one appears on the screen

1:45:26 Two men exit George's and turn to their right.

That's north, away from the alley where Collin was killed.

1:49:10   Two women exist George's and wait outside. A car arrives. They get in and the car drives off.

1:55:02   Two women exit George's and turn to their left.
          South. Toward the alley.

1:59:19   One man exits George's, stands outside, and then walks across the street and out of the video.

2:00:01   Four men exit George's and walk across the street, eventually out of the video.

Detective Harding stopped the video.

"You will see Collin come out next," Detective Harding forewarned Lauren. She took some deep breaths and nodded. Detective Harding started the video.

2:00:31   Collin started to exit George's but paused in the doorway.

"You can see that he's laughing but no one else is visible. We don't know if he was talking to someone inside the bar or just laughing to himself."

2:00:40 – 2:00:45 Collin exited the bar and turned to the left.
          South.

2:01:05   Four men exit George's. They pause and look to the left and to the right as they talk. Two of the men turn to their right.
          North.
          The other two men go left.
          South.

2:01:35   A man exits George's. He looks to his left and to his right, eventually turning left.

South.

Over the next five minutes, five more men and five more women exit George's and get into various cars or walk away. Then the lights from the bar go out and Detective Harding stopped the video.

Lauren let out a loud exhale and leaned back into her seat. She looked at Detective Harding.

"How many of these people did you interview?"

"We got as many names as we could. We looked at credit card receipts from the bar and put out a public request for anyone who was leaving George's that night after 1:30am. In the end, we were able to question that group of four men at 2:01:05 and the single man at 2:01:35."

"That's right, I remember," Lauren lied. "But tell me again, what were their stories?"

"The group of four are locals. Monthly guys'-night-out kind of thing. They're regulars at George's. No priors. The single guy was our prime suspect. Had a rap sheet a mile long but nothing serious. Petty stuff really. His lawyer got involved pretty quickly. The only DNA evidence on Collin that night was Collin's own. We never recovered a weapon and there were no witnesses. So, since we couldn't get anything to stick on him for Collin, we had to release him. We kept eyes on him but he actually got arrested the next month. Seems he stepped up his game."

"What happened in January?" Lauren asked.

"Arrested and charged with 1st degree murder of a successful local business owner. It was pretty big news for a while. But a witness' ID was always a bit iffy and there was no other way to connect him to the scene or credible motive. His lawyer eventually got the charges dropped."

Lauren sat in silence. She'd seen everyone's faces but no one looked familiar. Or even suspicious. Rising from her chair, Lauren extended her hand.

"Thanks very much, Detective. I really appreciate your time and the trouble in setting this up for me."

Detective Harding shook her hand.

"You're welcome, Ms. Brown. Take care of yourself."

Lauren left the precinct that afternoon with mixed emotions.

I've seen their faces. But who did it?

Tears began to well up in her eyes as she slowly made her way down the sidewalk. About two blocks later it dawned on her.

I know how to solve this! I know how to find out who killed Collin! Why didn't I think of this earlier?!

Picking up the pace, she headed home and began to plan her steps for the next five months - May to December.

It was 5:30pm when she arrived back at the apartment. As she entered, she sang out, "Hi, honey. I'm home!" and smiled to herself.

She had a plan.

Chapter 10 - Family

As the days in May turned toward April, Lauren found herself surprised at how quickly she'd settled into the role of playing Theo's girlfriend, including their romantic relationship. Early on, she had successfully avoided any potential interaction that could be misconstrued as sexual. Never instigating affection and never undressing in his line of sight. But once it was early May, she realized she couldn't keep that up indefinitely.

This is my reality now. I still love Collin but I'll be more successful in finding out what happened to him if I stay with Theo and eventually see how everything plays out. And that means being here, with him, as his girlfriend.

As it turned out, Theo's work was really feast or famine. It was either 70-hour weeks or less than 40. And the longer she lived in the apartment, the 70-hour weeks became the norm. His text messages were frequent and predictable:

Theo: *Sorry, wrapping up a big M&A deal tonight. Don't stay up.*

Or

Theo: *I'm swamped. Eat without me.*

That was just fine with Lauren.

He's made it easy for me, she admitted to herself. *The perks are real. He's handsome, has a great job, a great apartment and I've got plenty of time on my own.*

Another real perk to being with Theo, it turned out, was that he was a real family man. The photos in the apartment were sweet, of course, but Lauren had no way of knowing exactly how important family was to him until his alarm went off at 6:30am on Saturday, May 4.

Lauren yawned through her question, "What's that for?"

"Come on, get up. Remember, we're headed to Summit for the day. Parker and Steph are expecting us this morning!"

What?

Lauren almost laughed out loud.

What did I have to agree to for this to happen?

But she didn't complain a bit, jumping out of bed with a, "Yeah!"

Showering quickly, she was almost giddy with excitement at the idea of spending the day with her family without having to play the peacemaker between two grown men - something she always had to do whenever Collin and Parker were together.

Less than two hours later, Theo and Lauren were taking presents out of the bedroom closet, bottles of wine out of the kitchen, and loading them all into his car.

The Stall

This should be interesting, Lauren thought, realizing she had no idea what gifts she'd bought for her nieces.

I assume I bought them, because Theo wouldn't know what to get the girls. Guess I'll find out soon.

Lauren smiled to herself.

The ride to Summit was relatively short and it went by even more quickly with Theo's non-stop questions.

"So, any landmines I should avoid?"

Landmines? What does he mean?

She gave him a strange look.

"Landmines. Things I should avoid asking or bringing up. You mentioned he can be sensitive."

Ahhhhhhhhhh. This will be the first time Parker and Theo ever meet. Oh man...

All of a sudden Lauren was the nervous one.

"Well, ok, there are a few. He never approved of me leaving New Jersey and moving to Chelsea, so avoid that. He wanted me to move back and I obviously never did, so avoid that. He thinks I wasted my chance to graduate from art school and he definitely thinks making lattes for other people is a waste of my life. Those are the big tickets. That enough?"

Lauren rattled off the list with a smile in her voice.

"Lauren, I knew all of that already. You told me that months ago."

Shit, of course. I probably already gave him my family's history. Quick, think of new ones!

"Oh sorry. Duh. It's early, not enough coffee."

Theo just smiled at her and waited for her to continue.

"Ok, Parker and his wife are really nice people. They're easy to get along with, I think, as long as you keep the conversation light and obviously avoid those topics from the past. Parker loves talking football, loves the Giants. So, no teasing. And Steph is a great mom. Works from home in an IT job. I can't really say anything bad about her."

"Ok! Football. Working mother. Great kids. Easy!" Theo beamed at her as they pulled into Parker's neighborhood. "Thanks for the Brown family primer!"

The rest of the day was like a dream for Lauren. As soon as Steph opened their front door, the house erupted in screams of delight and more hugs than Lauren had ever seen given under one roof.

"Lauren!" Parker and Steph chimed in together.

"Auntie Lauren!" the two girls yelled together as they dashed by their parents and grabbed Lauren's legs, bouncing up and down.

"Come here!" Parker called out, trying to speak over the laughing girls, and he reached out to embrace Lauren with a heartfelt hug.

"And this must be Theo!" Parker said as he shook Theo's hand sincerely. He motioned toward the driveway. "Come on, let's get out of this craziness and I'll help you unload the car."

A few minutes later, Parker and Theo walked into the house carrying suitcases, gifts and wine. The girls practically tackled Theo before Parker came to his defense.

"Girls, back up, back up, and give the man some space or he may keep all those presents for himself!" This sent the girls into another bouncing, giggling fit.

The Stall

Within the hour the girls were sitting on the floor of their living room tearing open the gift bags and wrapped boxes. After each gift was opened, they'd run over and give Lauren a big hug with calls of, "Thank you for the dolls!" and "Thank you for the toys!" Lauren was almost overcome by the joy in that room. And from the look on Theo's face, he was loving it as much as she was.

Lauren caught herself deep in thought.

Why couldn't Parker and Collin put their differences behind them? We could have had days like this together.

Parker must have read her mind because after the noise died down and the girls ran off to play with their toys, he asked Lauren to follow him out onto their deck.

"You doing ok?" he asked, closing the door behind them.

Lauren smiled, "Yeah. Just thinking."

"I get it," Parker stepped toward Lauren and wrapped his arms around her. "I'm so glad you're here. It's been too long, sister. And I'm so glad you brought Theo. We're so happy to finally meet him. He really is great."

Lauren smiled over Parker's shoulder, "Yeah, he really is. Thanks. I've missed you guys. Really missed the girls."

Lauren sighed.

Might as well be truthful.

"And it was never this lighthearted before. I regret that."

Parker stepped back and leaned against the railing.

"Lauren, you shouldn't regret anything. It was all on me and Collin. You did nothing wrong."

Lauren nodded.

Ok. Here's my chance to set the record straight.

"I know you didn't agree with my choices after leaving school, Parker, but I want you to know that leaving and moving to Chelsea were *my* choices. And Collin had nothing to do with me staying there. He loved me and I loved him. We had a *good* life."

And with the word *good*, the slightest crack in her voice emerged.

"Oh, Lauren. We were both just kids when Mom and Dad died. I mean, you *were* a kid and I was barely an adult. I never dreamed you'd drop out of college and then literally leave me behind. It hurt. So. Much. And I loved you too much to blame *you*, so I blamed Collin."

Parker's voice was the one wavering now.

"Everything that happened in December was awful. Just awful. And seeing how happy the girls were when you got here today makes me regret not making more of an effort on my part. But I can't go back in time, Lauren."

How ironic to hear that.

"So, anyway, Steph and I are really happy to know you've moved on. Theo's really great."

"Thanks for saying all that, Parker. That means a lot."

Just then, Steph stuck her head out the door and smiled at them.

"Lunch is ready. You coming in or are we coming out?"

Parker gave Lauren one more hug and then they walked toward the door.

"Let's eat, I'm starved."

Just as they entered the kitchen, Parker added, "So, Theo, you like football?"

Theo smiled and winked at Lauren as if to say, *I got this.*

Chapter 11 – A New Normal

The trip to see Parker, Steph and the girls was more than Lauren could have wished for and she rode that high for weeks in the month of April and late March. Although it wouldn't be able to repair the rift that had existed between Parker and Collin, hearing her brother say he regretted not making an effort with him made her feel much better.

Between work, seeing Abbie and the occasional night out with Theo, time passed pretty quickly for Lauren. She and Theo even had Cam and Kelly over for a few dinner parties. The first one for Lauren was going to be Saturday, March 16, and she was nervous.

Even though Lauren and Theo had met with up Cam a few times for drinks since May, hosting him and Kelly for dinner that night in March felt different. It was one thing to talk over glasses of wine and it never lasted more than an hour or so. Dinner would be a longer affair.

Lauren had become skilled in participating in conversations – *just* on the surface - with enough of a light-touch that the other person never noticed the lack of details. Keeping her comments limited to the '4 W's' as she called them - Wine, Work, Wardrobe and Weather – she left the backstories and inside jokes to the others and things usually stayed comfortable. But with Cam, she was nervous.

Would Theo's oldest friend see through me or pick up on something just a bit 'off'?

Around 6:30pm that evening, dinner was almost ready when Theo and Kelly walked over to the windows to look down onto the city lights. That left Cam and Lauren in the kitchen. Cam had just opened the second bottle of wine for the evening.

"Here you are," he said as he handed a glass to Lauren.

"Thanks. It was really nice of you to bring the wine this evening, Cam. How did you know this was my favorite?"

Cam smiled and motioned his head toward Theo, still standing at the windows talking to Kelly.

"Someone told me."

"Ah. Of course," Lauren smiled. "He thinks of everything, doesn't he?"

"He does, with YOU."

Lauren gave him a puzzled look.

"What do you mean?"

Cam put his glass down on the kitchen island.

"You know, Lauren, I've been friends with Theo a long time. And that whole time, he's had his share of girlfriends. Some were nice. Some were terrible," Cam laughed. "Honestly, terrible! And even if he wasn't *officially* dating anyone, he was *always* talking about someone. And then somehow you come along…and then it was nonstop. This woman at Starbucks is *so beautiful*. This woman at Starbucks is *so kind*. I finally had to tell him to either ask you out or stop talking about you! And I'm glad he finally *did* ask you because things are, well, different with you. I've never seen him as happy as he is right now. It's like he's finally able to be himself."

Lauren was at a complete loss for words. All she could do was smile.

Wow. Cam really is a good guy.

"I hope you're as happy as he is, Lauren. What you guys have is really special."

"Thank you, Cam. That is really nice to hear. I am happy *and* lucky. Theo is a great guy."

Lauren raised her glass to toast with Cam. Just then, Theo and Kelly walked toward the kitchen.

"What are we toasting to?" Kelly asked.

"To Theo and Lauren, the perfect couple," Cam replied.

"I'll drink to that!" Theo raised a glass to Lauren and kissed her.

Lauren worked a shift at the café on Friday, March 15th and had just left the cafe around 2:00pm when she got a text from Theo.

Theo: *Hi! Text me when you get home. Love you!*

Another late night. No problem. Lauren thought to herself.

"Good afternoon, Ms. Brown," the doorman greeted her as she approached the front of the apartment.

It had always bothered Lauren that she didn't know his first name.

Can't exactly ask him at this point, she thought, so she stuck with, "Hello, how are you?"

"Very well, thank you. Ms. Brown, there are a number of packages that arrived today and need to be delivered up to your apartment. Would you like me to have them brought up now or later perhaps?"

"Packages? Well, sure, now is fine."

Odd, I haven't ordered anything. Probably for Theo.

"Wonderful, I'll have them brought up."

Ten minutes later, the apartment doorbell rang and Lauren opened the door. In the hall in front of her was a luggage rack stacked with boxes, a suitcase, and tote bags. She recognized everything immediately.

My stuff.

She let out a long exhale.

"Um, please come in," she said as she motioned for the porter to wheel the rack into the apartment. "I guess you can stack everything over there," she added as she motioned to the far wall of the living room.

Looking down into the top box, she pulled out a picture frame. Her and Collin's smiling faces looked back at her. Taken at some outside café, they were saying 'cheers' to the photographer with wine and beer in their hands.

This was about a year ago.

And then suddenly it hit her.

It's happening. My stuff is here. That means any day now I'll move out of my old place. And the day before that, I'll be living there.

Lauren looked down at the box again, finding more photographs and books. She stood in a daze, not sure how she felt.

Keep your mind on the goal. You want to get back home and eventually back to December.

The Stall

A phone call brought her back around. It was Theo.

"Hey, you were supposed to text me when you got home."

"Oh, sorry. Hey, all my stuff is here."

"Awesome, I was hoping it had arrived. We can go through it all tonight and sort out the stuff we don't need. Most of it can be trashed."

Wait, what?

Although Lauren understood what he meant, hearing it put *that* way stung. He sounded callous. Lauren stayed silent as her fingers tightened their grip around the picture frame.

Theo must have picked up on it because he quickly backtracked.

"Um, I mean we can sort through it and put into storage what you don't want right now. Keep whatever you want. I just meant, like, you won't need kitchen stuff and old clothes, you know."

"And my furniture?"

"Still over there. The new renters kept it all, remember?"

Lauren tried to keep her head straight.

Don't panic, you'll be living back home soon with all your stuff, your furniture AND these pictures. VERY soon.

"Yes, of course. Thanks."

"K, gotta go. But I'm very excited. Big step! Love you!" Theo said and then hung up.

Lauren looked at all the boxes again.

I haven't seen any of my photos or books in Theo's apartment before. We must have decided to put it all into storage.

And with that, she ran her fingers over the photo of Collin's face before putting it back into the box and resealing the tape. Everything would wait for Theo to come home and then be taken away.

As Lauren expected, she awoke on Thursday, March 14, to find the boxes were not in Theo's apartment. Walking to work later that morning, she realized she was going to have to figure out the date when she actually moved *into* Theo's apartment so she would show up when he expected her.

How do I figure that out? Maybe Abbie can help.

She sent a quick text.

Lauren: *Hi, guess what?*

Abbie didn't waste any time replying.

Abbie: *What?*
Lauren: *I'm officially OUT of my old place. My stuff will arrive tomorrow!*
Abbie: *AWESOME!!! So happy for you!!*
Lauren: *Thanks! Time is flying, huh? Feels like I just got here.*

Come on, Abbie, take the bait. Please. Lauren said to herself.

Abbie: *Yup. Guess that's what love does to you XOXOXOXOXO*

Give me more. Lauren drummed her fingers on the phone screen. She didn't have to wait long.

The Stall

Abbie: *I bet you're REALLY glad your lease went month to month for 2024. I know your rent was higher but I remember you wanted the flexibility, you know, to move out if you needed to get away from it all.*

Lauren: *You're right. I needed the ability to move out if I needed to... after Collin died. I'm glad I did it, too.*

Lauren exhaled deeply.

Abbie: *Yes and doing that made it easy for you to vacate at the end of Feb! Now look where you are, Miss Penthouse. Oh wait. LOL, not like THAT!*

Lauren didn't even pick up on the joke.
END OF FEBRUARY. *It's not an exact date but it's a ballpark.*

Lauren: *K. Gotta go make room for my stuff. TTYL.*

Lauren ended the text and looked at the calendar on her phone.
Most likely I moved in with Theo around February 29th. Leap Day. Quite a leap indeed, brave girl.

Chapter 12 - Thomas

The next ten days flew by quickly, moving toward the beginning of March. Lauren kept her eyes and ears open for clues from Theo, hoping he'd mention the *exact* date she had moved in, but he hadn't said anything specific. By Tuesday, March 5, she was thinking February 29 was most likely her move-in day. As it turned out, the still nameless doorman provided the confirmation she needed.

"Good morning, Ms. Brown," he greeted her in his usual friendly manner as she exited the building that morning.

"Good morning," Lauren replied and paused on the sideway, looking left and right, trying to *appear* as if she was getting her bearings.

"May I assist with directions somewhere?"

"No, I think I'm ok. Just figuring out which way is north!"

The doorman smiled at her and pointed to his left.

"Yes, it does take a while. Is there anything I can do to help you get settled in?"

My *opening*.

"All settled, actually."

The Stall

"Already? That's impressive! It has only been five days."

Five days...I've been here five days. My lease ends February 29 so that means I move in here the same day.

Lauren smiled and then quickly thought to add, "Apologies, but with everything going on, my brain's a bit full. Would you please remind me of your name again?"

He smiled at her kindly.

"No apologies needed. I'm Thomas Davidson. Everyone calls me Thomas."

"Thank you, Thomas. See you again soon!" Lauren smiled to herself as she walked away.

Yes, thank you, Thomas!

When her alarm went off on the morning of Friday, March 1, Lauren had a plan in place. She'd purposely set it a bit early so she could see Theo before he left for work and play the 'excited new roommate' role she knew he'd expect. Rolling over, she found him already awake, looking at her.

"Well, good morning," she said, surprised to find him a few inches from her face.

"Good morning, roomie. Sleep well?"

"Ummmm, yes. Very well. This bed is incredible. A lot better than my old one."

Lauren wasn't lying. The mattress she and Collin had slept on hadn't been cheap but it wasn't nearly as luxurious and comfortable as Theo's.

Theo propped himself up on one arm and leaned down to kiss her, adding, "Good. First night of many, sweetheart."

Lauren smiled back at him.

"Listen, I've gotta go. Visiting a client north of the park at 9:00am. But maybe tonight we can go out to celebrate your first full day as a resident here."

"Sounds great. I work today. Off at 5:00pm."

"Ok. Tell Abbie hi. I'm sure her brain is about to explode with questions for you."

Theo winked at her and kissed her one more time.

"I make a full carafe of coffee each morning, so look for it in the kitchen."

Lauren watched him get up and head towards the bathroom.

"Yea, it's amaz...," Lauren stopped herself from blurting out *it's amazing.*

Shit. Think quick!

"Ok, I'm sure it'll be amazing. Thanks!"

Lauren stared at the ceiling, chastising herself.

Really? After all this time, you almost blew it.

Within 30 minutes, Theo had dressed and left the apartment. Lauren let out a sigh of relief. Her mind turned to the next day - the last day of February - when she'd be back inside her old apartment. As nice as Theo's place was, she was ready to be back in her own space. Home.

I can let my guard down there. It'll be easier to be Theo's girlfriend when I'm in my own space. And I've got to get my head ready for what's coming... eventually... in December.

With a smile on her face, she got up to get ready for work.

The Stall

Lauren had barely stepped through Starbuck's front door later that morning when Abbie spied her and started in.

"Heyyyyyyyyyy. How was it?"

"First night? Great!" Lauren replied, raising her eyebrows seductively and smiling at Abbie.

That's what she wants to hear.

For the rest of her shift, Lauren alternated between dark roasts, chai lattes, and Abbie's unending questions.

After work, Theo kept his promise to take Lauren out for dinner and a walk around her new neighborhood. After they settled back inside the apartment, they snuggled together on the sofa with a glass of wine, looking out onto the city lights.

"Here's to our new future," Theo toasted.

Future and past.

"Here's to us," Lauren smiled as she leaned over to kiss Theo.

Chapter 13 - Moving Day

Lauren actually had trouble falling asleep that evening next to Theo, too excited for what the next morning would bring. So, when daylight appeared on Thursday, February 29th, she opened her eyes and immediately shot up in bed.

"YES!!!!!" Lauren yelled and drummed the bed with her fists. Her bed. Her bedroom. Her pillows and blankets. She fell back onto her pillow and took a deep breath.

"Home."

Time for the tour.

She got out of bed and headed toward the door. Walking out into the hall, she almost tripped over the half-full boxes that sat just outside the bedroom door.

Yup, guess today is moving day.

Her excitement of being home drained a bit, realizing she would still be packing her life into those boxes and heading to Theo's that day.

But I'll be back.

Around 12:00pm, Theo called.

"Hi! How's the packing going?"

"Oh, fine. Just packing up some photos and other small stuff now."

"Great. The moving guys I booked are coming over in a few hours to take your car and boxes to storage. When do you have to be out?"

"5 o'clock."

"Ok, that's good. I'll leave work early and pick you and your suitcases up at 4."

"Sounds great, but I'm not bringing much," Lauren replied.

I'm going to see it all soon anyway.

She hesitated for another moment and then added, "Love you."

"Love you too!" Theo replied and hung up.

Lauren hung up and laughed to herself. If she were eight years old, she'd have her fingers crossed behind her back.

Love? Just the next stage of the game, brave girl. If I'm gonna see this through, I've gotta lay it on thick.

Right on time, her apartment intercom rang at 4:00pm and Lauren buzzed Theo through. Arriving at her door a moment later, he found Lauren and her two suitcases ready to go.

"This is it?"

"Yup, think so," Lauren said. "Just the necessities for this lady. Furniture stays."

"No worries. The boxes that the movers picked up earlier will stay in storage until we have a place for them. They'll bring it to the apartment later."

Yes, I know.

And with that, he picked up her suitcases and Lauren locked the door behind them.

See you soon.

Chapter 14 - February

In many ways, the next 14 days were the happiest Lauren had spent in months. Each day she'd wake up in her own apartment and fill her days doing exactly what she wanted to - working, hanging out with Abbie and roaming her neighborhood. On a few occasions, she even ran into Mrs. Adams in the hallway, stopping to exchange hellos and talk about the weather.

On one particularly cold and icy February morning, Lauren was headed out of the building when she heard Mrs. Adams coming down the stairs. Lauren stayed inside the doorway while Mrs. Adams approached.

"Hello, Mrs. Adams. Are you headed out in this weather?"

"Oh yes, I need milk. Just going around to the corner market."

"Why don't you let me pick it up for you. I'm headed that way for some coffee and they haven't salted the icy sidewalks yet."

"Oh, that would be wonderful. Thank you so much, Lauren. Here, let me give you five dollars," Mrs. Adams replied as she reached into her purse. Lauren put out her hand to stop her.

"Don't mention it. It will be my pleasure. Whole, two percent or skim?"

A few minutes later, Lauren had purchased the milk and her coffee and was headed back home when she almost slipped twice on the ice. She was glad that she'd seen Mrs. Adams before the elderly lady had gone outside by herself. Arriving at the entrance to their building, she saw the landlord, Mr. Davis, coming out with a bucket and scoop. Lauren smiled at him and was relieved to see he was putting out salt.

"Good morning, Lauren," Mr. Davis greeted her. "I'm sorry I wasn't out here earlier. Be careful."

"Thank you, I will. And you too!"

A few moments later, Mrs. Adams met Lauren at her apartment door and was all smiles as she took the milk from her.

"Thank you again, Lauren. You were a life saver today!"

"You're very welcome. And please promise me you won't go outside for a while. Mr. Davis is just now putting down salt."

Mrs. Adams promised she would stay inside until it was safe and said goodbye.

Back inside her own apartment, Lauren sat down and sipped her coffee by the window, chastising herself for not checking in on her neighbor more frequently and made a mental note to do so.

It wasn't long before her thoughts turned to Collin – and what was coming.

I've got about 9 weeks until the day Collin is killed. Do I just show up in the alley and stop it?

Lauren shook her head at the thought of that.

The Stall

The only thing I know for certain is that every morning when I wake up, I'm one day closer. And I've got to believe I'm in this crazy, backwards cycle for a reason. Just take it a day at a time and believe that I'll figure it out.

On the morning of Valentine's Day, Lauren awoke to a text - from Theo, of course - prepping her for some outdoor, but secret, romantic plans. Lauren laughed out loud as she thought about the day ahead and Theo's upcoming invitation to move in.

He's sweet. Even though I know what's coming, I'll act sooooo surprised.

Dressed in jeans and a sweater, she met him downstairs at 1:00pm.

"Ready?" he asked as she got in his car.

"Ready! And where exactly are we going?" Lauren smiled at him.

"It's a beautiful day. I thought we should get out and see some parts of the city you may not have seen before."

"Ok, but I've been around a lot. You taking me to the Bronx?" Lauren laughed.

"Nope."

And with that, Theo gave a 'my lips are sealed' motion with his fingers. Lauren sat back.

Ok, I'm intrigued.

Within 30 minutes, Theo had weaved from Chelsea to the East River and eventually pulled into a parking lot. The sign read *NY Copters*.

Lauren's head was on a swivel between looking at Theo and the helicopters visible on the side of the lot.

"Are you serious? Oh my God, Theo!"

"Happy Valentine's Day! Are you surprised?"

"Surprised? Yes!"

"Ok, let's go! I told you we were going to see some parts of the city you hadn't seen before."

The next hour was like a dream for Lauren. Starting off, the pilot took them south over the Statue of Liberty, lower Manhattan and then followed the Hudson River north. Theo and Lauren both tried to make out her building.

"There! No, there!" they both called out back and forth until they eventually gave up, laughing hysterically into their headsets.

Heading toward Central Park, Lauren couldn't believe her eyes as she looked down on top of the city she'd called home... with Collin.

He would have loved this.

Lauren pushed the thought out of her mind, not wanting to dampen the moment, and allowed herself to be present, here, enjoying this gift.

Maybe I earned the right to enjoy this.

After so many loops and turns, Lauren completely lost track of where they were.

"This is amazing. Kinda bad to say most buildings look the same from up here," she said to Theo, laughing.

"Know that place?" he asked, pointing past her shoulder and down toward a tall building. She shook her head.

"You've been there."

Lauren shook her head again.

"That's my place!"

Of course! So THIS is how he's going to ask.

"Ah! It looks a little different from up here but still *very* impressive," she added jokingly.

The Stall

"Lauren," Theo turned toward her in his seat. "Things are going so well for us. You've made me the happiest man alive and I can't stand being apart from you. I'd really love it if you'd move in with me. This can be your home, too."

Surprised. Act surprised.

"Really?"

"Yes, really," Theo laughed at her.

"Yes, yes, 1000 percent, yes!"

Right on cue, the pilot motioned behind him to a cooler sitting near Theo. Lauren watched as Theo opened it and pulled out a chilled bottle of champagne and two flutes.

"Here's to our new future," Theo toasted.

This sounds familiar.

"Here's to us."

Chapter 15 - Abbie

Time was passing quickly for Lauren, thanks to Theo. As early February eventually turned into late January, she had to admit that Theo knew how to spoil a woman. Dinners, flowers and gifts had become a weekly occurrence and it felt, well, nice. Lauren hadn't seen this much attention since when she and Colllin first began dating. Even her coworkers thought it was sweet, smiling when they saw him walk in multiple times a week, and always requesting that Lauren take his order. Everyone thought it was romantic...except Abbie. By Monday, January 15th, she spoke up.

"Wow, he's kinda in here all the time, Lauren. Isn't that creepy to you?"

Lauren laughed.

Creepy? No. Maybe strange. I could tell you stories about strange.

"Really? No, I think it's sweet. And isn't he handsome?"

Abbie smiled and nodded, "Well, I guess that's true."

"Everything's ok. Really. But thank you."

"I just wanted to say something because...," Abbie trailed off.

"Because it's only been a month," Lauren finished Abbie's sentence.

She could see the tears in Abbie's eyes.

"Yeah."

"Oh Abbie," Lauren reached out her arms and gave her friend a long, strong hug. "Thank you. Thank you for watching out for my heart. But I'm ok. Everything's ok, I promise. I like Theo. He's kind, funny, and he's been good for me. I'm not sure if I've *officially* moved on, but..." Lauren paused for effect. "I'm going to have to, eventually."

"Oh honey. I know. I really do! It's just that after all the press around Collin and you, I just wanted to make sure he's not some weirdo. I swear to God, you let me know if you get any vibes that he's after your..." Abbie stopped mid-sentence.

"My what?"

Abbie let out a deep sigh. "Money, Lauren. Your inheritance. You remember the local press after Collin died? They made a big deal about your family. How it was so tragic that you'd lost your parents and then Collin. They wrote about your inheritance. How you were some rich New Jersey girl living in the city. It was awful! And it wasn't fair. Like having money made it less tragic for you to lose Collin."

Lauren's face immediately fell.

Press? About my inheritance? No, no, no, no. No way had Theo found his way into her life because of that.

Lauren shook her head at Abbie.

"Hey, um, I've gotta get back to work. Thanks, really, but it's fine. He's fine. We're fine."

And with that, she turned away from her friend and walked back to the counter.

"Next customer, please."

Abbie's comments had certainly given Lauren something to think about that afternoon.

This can't be true. Can it? And even if he did see the coverage and knew I had my own money, what did that mean? Anything?

Ironically, Theo arrived just as her shift ended at 5:00pm and officially asked her out on their first date.

So, this is when the romance starts.

Lauren accepted and they went out for dinner.

Chapter 16 – Cam

The conversation with Abbie in mid-January had shaken Lauren so badly, that for days her mind was flooded with the countless conversations she'd had with Theo since June. Nothing seemed odd. Nothing seemed off.

So maybe the fact that he asked me out in January seemed a bit too soon for Abbie, but he's incredibly successful. Great job. Great apartment. My financial security couldn't have anything to do with him eventually asking me out. Could it?

Lauren went to work on Monday, January 8th convinced Abbie was just being over-protective. As expected, Theo appeared in line that morning at 7:45am.

"Hi, Theo! How are you?"

"Hi Lauren, great! How are you doing?"

"Same! What can I get you?"

"The usual."

Lauren entered his order into the computer: Grande, medium roast, black.

Looking up at him, she asked, "To go, right?"

"Actually, no. I'll have it here."

She wrote his name on a cup and Theo paid.

"I'm going on break soon so I'll bring it over to you if you can wait a few," Lauren smiled.

"Sure!" Theo looked over his shoulder and motioned to an empty table. "I'll be over there."

Five minutes later, Lauren walked up to his table and placed the cup in front of Theo.

"Your java, sir."

It took Theo a few seconds to look up from his phone.

"Oh hey, thanks! Wow, table service. Don't let the other guys in here see you or else they'll expect the same thing!"

Lauren laughed.

"Nope, you just had good timing. May I sit?"

"Please!" Theo put his phone to the side.

"Did I interrupt something? I can go if you're...."

Theo cut her off.

"Oh no, no biggie. Just reading this article," Theo turned the phone around so Lauren could see the screen. "It's about my best friend. We met during undergrad. He works for a big firm here in the city and just got charges dropped for one of his clients. I've gotta call him later so we can go celebrate!"

Lauren looked down and read the headline.

CHARGES DON'T STICK FOR ACCUSED NEW YEARS' KILLER

She knew the attorney's name without even reading it. Cameron.

The Stall

Act surprised.

"That's good for his client, I guess."

"Yeah! And good for the firm. Hey, you should meet him sometime."

Actually, I already have.

"Sure, sounds great!"

"You know, he's around here sometimes. Let me show you a picture of him, just in case he comes in."

Theo scrolled through the article.

"Sure," Lauren said politely, fully aware of what Cam looked like.

Theo handed the phone to Lauren and she looked down at the photo, expecting to see the typical professional headshot of Cam. Instead, she saw Cam standing at a microphone while a man stood behind him, grinning at the camera.

Lauren read the caption:

Defense Attorney Cameron Thomas Young addresses the press after his client, Jonathan Michael Jones, is released from police custody.

Lauren immediately dropped the phone.

"Hey, are you ok?" Theo asked, reaching for his phone. Lauren was silent.

Standing behind Cam, all smiles, was the man Lauren had seen leaving George's by himself in the surveillance video. Detective Harding's prime suspect. And, quite possibly, Collin's killer.

Lauren's mind raced back to her meeting with Detective Harding.

"*...had a rap sheet a mile long but nothing serious. Petty stuff really.... we were keeping an eye on him but he actually got arrested the next month...arrested and charged with 1st degree murder... local business owner with lots of money...pretty*

81

big news for a while. Witness ID was iffy... His lawyer eventually got the charges dropped."

Lauren quickly sat back in the chair and put her hand to her mouth in silent disbelief.

This man. His lawyer is Cam. Theo's best friend! Is there a connection? Oh my God.

Theo was concerned.

"Hey, are you ok? Sorry to be cliche, but you look like you've seen a ghost."

"No, um, I'm fine. Sorry. Just something on my mind."

Change the freaking topic.

"So, tell me about how you and Cam met."

Theo started rambling about his best friend, classes and parties. All Lauren could do was smile as she tried to quiet the bile churning in her stomach.

Keep it together. If there's a connection to Theo somehow, you've got to keep up this façade until you figure it out.

Chapter 17 - Jonathan Michael Jones

A quick Google search on Wednesday, January 3rd, told Lauren everything she needed to know about Jonathan Michael Jones and why he was arrested.

LIQUOR STORE KINGPIN FOUND SHOT NYE

ARREST IN LIQUOR STORE MURDER AFTER WITNESS COMES FORWARD

LIQUOR KILLER LAWYERS UP

From the articles, Lauren learned the basics: Mr. Frank Alzar, the owner of a chain of very successful liquor stores, was found shot after midnight on January 1st. A resident in a nearby apartment did not hear anything but claimed to see a man matching Jones' description flee the scene. Well-known defense attorney, Cameron Thomas Young, was brought in almost immediately after the arrest. Through his attorney, Jones proclaimed his innocence, stating that he was at a party across town that night and nowhere near the liquor store. Mr. Young says it is a case of mistaken identity.

"And so they had to release him," Lauren said to herself as she opened a bottle of wine.

For the next few minutes, she sat on the sofa with a journal and pen, writing out everything she had learned in the prior 14 days.

Abbie questioned Theo's motives with me – Money?
Jonathan Michael Jones kills store owner January 1st
Jones's lawyer is Theo's best friend – Connection?

Then Lauren scribbled out what *would* happen:

I meet Theo – Where? When?
Press coverage about my inheritance
Funeral December 18th
Press coverage about Collin's murder
Police interview me
Police come tell me Collin is dead
Collin is murdered December 11th
I hit my head at George's December 10th

Lauren swirled the red wine in her glass, reading, and re-reading, her list.

I've got to decide where to focus my time. I can't control where and when I meet Theo for the first time. I need to let that play out. And I can't control what the press writes about me.

Lauren shut her eyes. Emotions flooded in.

But I need to get ready. The funeral. And the police interview. And when they come to my door. And on the night of Collin's murder do I...

Lauren opened her eyes.

Do I stop it?

She picked up her pen again and quickly added something to her list. Looking down at the page, she told herself, "I'm gonna need help with this."

Abbie questioned Theo's motives with me – Money?

Jonathan Michael Jones kills store owner January 1st

Jones's lawyer is Theo's best friend – Connection?

Find Jonathan Michael Jones. Can Detective Harding help me find him?

Chapter 18 – January 1, 2024

Lauren woke up on Monday, January 1st and a quick Google search of the city's online papers confirmed what she already knew. Mr. Frank Alzar had been found dead earlier that morning. A witness had identified Jones who had been taken into custody.

Suddenly, Lauren's cell phone rings. Parker! She had been so busy since she and Theo went to see him in May, she'd completely forgotten about reaching out to him.

She purposely let it ring a few times.

I've got to be careful here. Can't be too cheerful.

"Hi, Parker. Happy New Year."

"Hey, Lauren. Same to you. Am I interrupting something?"

"No, no, you're fine. What's up?"

"I just wanted to reach out and say hi. Tell you how much fun we had with you last week. It meant the world to the girls, Steph and me to have you here on Christmas Day."

Lauren made a mental note.

I go to their house for Christmas!

"Oh, thanks, Parker. It meant a lot to be together."

"Yeah. So, um, are you doing ok? I mean, gosh, it's only been 14 days."

Lauren quickly opened the calendar on her phone. Fourteen days prior was December 18th - the date of Collin's funeral.

"Yes, I'm fine. Being with you guys on Christmas made it a little easier."

"Yeah, ok. And I think this whole crap with the press seems to have died down. I still can't believe how they dug up everything about Mom and Dad's accident and our inheritance."

Lauren remembered Abbie's comments about how the press made a big deal about the wealth she and Parker had inherited.

"I'm glad it's behind us."

"Me too. Well, I'd better go. I'll do better about staying in touch. Promise."

"Me too. Thanks, Parker. I love you."

"I love you too, sis. Talk to you later."

Lauren hung up and started to make a Christmas gift shopping list, then stopped - and laughed to herself.

There's no use in buying anything today. It won't be here in the morning. I will just have to wait until the morning of the 25th to see what I've bought for them.

Chapter 19 – Christmas Day

She had barely turned off the car when Lauren heard screams of joy coming from inside the house. Parker, Steph and the girls were outside and helping unload the car within minutes.

"Auntie Lauren!!"

"Hey, sis. Merry Christmas!"

"Merry Christmas, girls! Merry Christmas, Parker! Hi Steph!"

Hugs all around.

For the next few hours, Lauren basked in the joy of Parker and Steph's family and the girls ripped open their presents, each one followed by a squeal of delight.

"My gosh, Lauren, you've spoiled them," Parker laughed as the girls ran off to play with their new toys.

Lauren knew her shopping spree could have been called extravagant, but she shrugged at him as if to say *hey, they're only young once.* In reality, she had actually surprised *herself* at what was in her closet that morning when she went to load the car.

The Stall

Man, I AM a great aunt!

Thanks to the amazing food, wine and conversation, she never once thought about Theo *or* Collin. That was, until she found herself wandering the hall of Parker's house, looking at family photographs that lined the walls. Staring at the beautiful images of her nieces as babies and other photographs taken over the past few years, she admitted a harsh truth to herself.

I've missed so much. And I wouldn't be here today if Collin were alive. There's no way he would have agreed. I'd tell myself it wasn't important and go along with whatever he wanted.

Looking at those photographs, Lauren was filled with regret.

Staying in Chelsea was my decision. But that didn't mean I had to completely disconnect from my family. How did I let that happen?

All of sudden, Lauren was pulled back into reality.

"Auntie Lauren!!! Let's make cookies!!"

She smiled to herself and walked toward the kitchen.

"Only if there are sprinkles!"

Chapter 20 - Mrs. Adams

Lauren's plans for Christmas Eve were simple: See if Detective Harding would be willing to help her find Jonathan Michael Jones.

I'm not sure he'll agree but it's the day before Christmas. Everyone will be in a good mood. Maybe.

Planning the conversation in her head, Lauren walked out of her apartment and turned to lock the door. Then suddenly she heard a thud and the low cry of a woman's voice coming from the apartment across the hall.

Mrs. Adams!

She ran across the hall and pounded on the door.

"Mrs. Adams! It's me, Lauren, from across the hall. Please open the door."

Lauren could hear a faint woman's voice say, "Oh, Lauren. It's fine. I just took a little tumble."

"No, please, Mrs. Adams. Open the door so I can check on you."

Eventually Lauren could hear Mrs. Adams' feet shuffle across the floor and toward the door. Very slowly, Mrs. Adams opened the door and peeked out.

The Stall

"I'm sorry to have startled you, dear. I'm completely fine."

Looking at Mrs. Adams' face, Lauren knew she was definitely not fine. A small drop of blood had begun to roll down Mrs. Adams' forehead.

"Mrs. Adams, you've cut yourself. Please let me in and I can help put a bandage on that."

"Oh, ok," Mrs. Adams agreed as she touched the drop of blood. She backed up and Lauren walked in.

"Here, please sit down," Lauren said as she motioned to a nearby chair. "I'll find a paper towel."

Lauren walked quickly into Mrs. Adams' kitchen and grabbed one from the roll on the countertop.

Handing it to Mrs. Adams, she asked, "Do you have bandages in your bathroom?"

"Yes, in the cabinet above the sink."

"Ok, I'll be right back."

As Lauren turned to walk down the hall, she realized she'd never been *inside* Mrs. Adams' apartment before. She'd only stood at the door when she delivered the milk in February. She noted the layout was a mirror image of her own, so finding the bathroom was easy.

"Here we are," Lauren said as she walked back into the front room. "Let's get this on you."

She stood in front of Mrs. Adams and applied the bandage quickly.

"Oh, thank you so much, Lauren. I'm quite embarrassed about this. I just caught my foot on the area rug. My daughter and grandson have been telling me to get rid of it. Said it was a tripping hazard. I guess they were right."

Then she looked up at Lauren with a very concerned look on her face.

"You won't tell them, will you?"

Lauren smiled at her, "Well, Mrs. Adams, I've never met them so I won't be able to contact them myself. But I think you should take some precautions like removing the rug. Next time might be more serious, you know. And perhaps have them get you one of those alert buttons that you wear around your neck. I've heard they work great and it's better to be safe than sorry."

Mrs. Adams smiled at her, visibly relieved that Lauren had no plans to tell her family about the fall.

"Thank you. That's a great idea. I'll do that."

Lauren smiled but silently scolded herself for not checking in on the elderly woman as frequently as she had intended. She looked around the room and noticed a large number of photos on the wall.

"This is a lovely apartment, Mrs. Adams. Is this your family?" She started to walk toward the images.

"Yes," Mrs. Adams pointed to a family grouping. "This is my daughter and her husband. And this is their son. He's an attorney at some big firm here in the city."

Lauren felt the color drain from her face as her stomach turned upside down. Smiling back at her was Theo.

Mrs. Adams turned to look at Lauren with a huge smile on her face.

"My goodness, I completely forgot to tell you! I told him about you a few months back. He was here visiting me and I asked if he was dating anyone. When he said no, I told him about you! I mentioned that you were a very nice young woman and that you worked at a coffee shop nearby. I *may* have mentioned you had a boyfriend living with you, I don't remember. Oh, and I guess maybe this wasn't any of my business, but I told him that he wouldn't need to worry about you dating him for *his* money. I told him about your big inheritance from your parents, God rest their souls."

Oh. My. God.

Lauren scrambled to find the right response.

"Well, um, Mrs. Adams, I appreciate you saying nice things about me. But how did you find out about my parents if you don't mind me asking."

"Oh, from Mr. Davis."

The landlord.

"I had been telling him what a nice neighbor you were. He went on to tell me how that was good to hear, considering the unfortunate events of your childhood. The conversation just went from there, I suppose."

The room started to spin and Lauren moved toward the apartment door.

"I...I'd better go now Mrs. Adams. Please be c-careful."

Within 30 seconds, Lauren was kneeling on her bathroom floor, vomiting into the toilet.

Chapter 21 - Christmas Eve

Lauren laid on the bathroom floor for over an hour, staring at the ceiling and processing what she had just learned. The fact that Mrs. Adams was Theo's grandmother, and that she had told Theo about Lauren and her inheritance, didn't *prove* anything. But what it did mean was that Theo knew about Lauren and where she lived months before Collin's murder. It would not have been difficult to find out exactly where she worked and that Collin lived with her.

The thought, *he pursued me,* raced through her mind and she shuddered.

Lauren's next steps were crystal clear now. She needed to talk to Jones. But she needed to find him first.

I need to make sure Detective Harding is working today before I put myself back together and go all the way over there on Christmas Eve.

Unfortunately, a few minutes later Lauren was told that Detective Harding had taken the day off. Just then, her phone rang. It was her manager asking her to come in. They needed backup. It was madness there. Lauren smiled, imagining how busy they must be on Christmas Eve.

The Stall

Fathers in need of coffee. Daughters in need of hot chocolate. All while out shopping for mom.

She was dressed and headed to work in thirty minutes.

Chapter 22 – The Customer

Madness didn't come close to describing work that day. And the same was true for December 23rd and 22nd. It seemed the entire population of New York City had procrastinated their gift buying. And they all needed caffeine. Or gift cards. Or coffee mugs. Or travel mugs. Or all four.

While Lauren was prepared for the throngs of tired, grouchy and thirsty customers cycling through the café, she was also prepared for how to treat Theo when he showed up. She knew he would.

His routine was almost comical, if not obsessive. Walking in, he would scan the café to see if she was at the counter. If she was, he would wait in line. Once at the front, he would make small talk, pay her a compliment, get his order, and leave. If she was clearing tables, he would stand back and wait for her to walk by. Then he would take his opportunity to say hello and smile. The thought that she might have found these actions cute, or even the slightest bit romantic, made her feel sick.

By December 21st, her coworkers' behavior made a dramatic shift. While at first their quick glances, sad smiles or text messages asking if she'd like them to cover her shift seemed odd, the reason eventually came to her:

Of course. Collin's funeral was December 18th.

So, on December 20th, she decided it was probably a good idea to stay home and prepare for the service, rather than worrying about how to act, or what to say, at work after burying your boyfriend. When the next text came in offering to take her shift, she replied with a simple, "*Thank you so much.*"

It was what people wanted to hear.

Chapter 23 - The Cemetery

When Lauren woke up on December 18th, her mind was already spinning.

She had spent the previous two days preparing to see everyone - Collin's parents, his brother and family, Parker, Steph and the girls, Abbie and other friends - and face their grief.

The thought, *I hope Collin's family doesn't hate me - yet,* had crossed her mind many times. But the biggest concern was seeing Collin's casket. There was no easy way to prepare for that.

Around 7:00am, Parker texted her to ask if she'd be ready for them to pick her up at 8:30am. From that, Lauren deduced she would ride with them to White Plains for the service.

A few moments before they arrived, Lauren spoke to herself in the mirror for one final pep talk.

"Ok, brave girl. No matter what happens, you're going to get through this. Today is temporary."

And with that, she heard Steph buzz the apartment intercom.

The Stall

"Lauren, honey. Are you ready?"

The drive was relatively nice. Parker had offered Lauren the front seat, but she declined and said she'd like to sit between her nieces in the back. Lauren enjoyed listening to the girls giggle as they each watched a video on an iPad. Every so often, one of them would look up at Lauren with a big smile on their face, point at the screen and laugh.

If Steph told the girls where they were going or why, they have already forgotten...thankfully.

Lauren smiled and kissed them both on top of their heads. That pleasantness, however, was short lived and dissolved completely as Parker pulled into the cemetery and rolled to a stop near the other cars.

Lauren's mind was racing.

Am I ready to face Collin's parents? What if his mother slaps me - or yells - or worse... ignores me?

Lauren did not have to wait long to find out.

Exiting Parker's car, Collin's mother and father were the first to walk toward Lauren. They held out their arms and together they embraced her tightly, their eyes red from tears already shed that morning. Feeling their arms around her, Lauren let out a deep breath and exhaled any worry of a confrontation or cold reception.

It was Parker who eventually separated them and suggested that everyone go take their seats. As Lauren turned to walk toward the chairs, she caught her breath as she saw Collin's casket for the first time.

Oh, Collin.

Parker immediately tuned into her line of sight and put a firm hand on her elbow.

"Come this way, sis."

A few moments later, Parker sat next to Lauren, then Steph and the girls. Alongside Parker were Collin's entire family. It was a solemn front row.

Lauren watched as her nieces kicked their legs back and forth on the chair, giggling quietly as they attempted to catch the snow piled under them and send it up into the air. Lauren smiled at them before Steph gave what must have been the world's worst mom-look. The girls immediately stopped.

No giggling was heard the rest of the day.

And so it began.

Chapter 24 - Aftermath

"It was a beautiful service."

"Such a nice service."

"We're so, so sorry."

"If you need anything..."

The sentiments echoed across the cemetery lawn. Lauren stopped listening. Numbness had set in and everyone knew it.

"Do you want to head home, Lauren?" Steph had one hand on Lauren's back and a wet tissue in the other. Lauren nodded.

"Ok, I'll go start the car to warm it up." Parker said quietly.

Lauren stood silently and watched Parker walk carefully through the snow toward the car. All of a sudden, something caught her eye. A man, about 30 yards beyond the cars, stood directly in her line of sight. It could have been just another man attending a different service or perhaps visiting a loved one's grave. But this was no random stranger to Lauren. She knew immediately who it was.

Theo.

Despite Parker and Steph's insistence that she spend the night in Summit, Lauren eventually found the words to convince them she wanted to be alone. Closing her apartment door, she leaned back against it and slid down to the floor. And there she sat and let out months of confusion, sheer loneliness and grief. And when she had exhausted those, she filled herself back up - with anger, danger and revenge.

Chapter 25 - The Press

It was barely dawn on December 17th when Lauren called the police station and asked if Detective Harding would be working. The man on the other end of the telephone confirmed that indeed, Detective Harding would be there from 10:00am-6:00pm today.

Great. I'll be there at 9:59am. First, I need coffee. Now.

Lauren decided not to go all the way to work for her own coffee, but instead stopped by the corner shop. It was a popular place for those who lived on the block and for those who didn't believe in supporting a large, global brand like her employer. Lauren gave this small shop as much business as she could, including her own coffee fix now and then.

"Good morning, Mrs. DeMartini," Lauren greeted the shop owner warmly and in return was given a long, comforting hug.

"Oh, Miss Lauren. I am so happy to see you. My family has been praying for you and Mr. Collin. We are absolutely heartbroken."

Lauren could see tears forming in Mrs. DeMartini's eyes.

"Thank you so much," Lauren took a deep breath. "May I please have a large black coffee."

Mrs. DeMartini smiled and said, "Yes, absolutely. And it is free for you today. Don't argue with me."

Lauren smiled back and nodded in agreement.

As Lauren waited for her coffee, she turned and looked around the shop. The usual, familiar items were there. Chips, granola bars, candy, small bottles of various toiletries, soda, water and the like. Lauren noticed a stand of magazines and newspapers just inside the door and walked over to them. She quickly regretted that decision. The newspaper headlines screamed the day's news. Three of them caught her eye.

CHELSEA MURDER VIC'S GIRLFRIEND WORTH MILLIONS

GRIEVING GIRLFRIEND INHERITED MILLIONS FROM PARENTS

SHE LOST PARENTS AND NOW TRUE LOVE

"Oh, Miss Lauren!" Mrs. DeMartini shouted across the shop to Lauren. "Get away from that trash! I told them not to display that horrible gossip in here."

Lauren turned and watched as the woman walked quickly across the shop floor with hot coffee in her hand. Lauren took the cup from her and turned her back to the newspapers.

"It's ok, Mrs. DeMartini. I'm pretty much numb to everything right now."

"Well, I don't want that trash in my shop until they move on to some other poor target!" She waved her arm toward the rack as if to wipe away their existence.

The Stall

"Thank you for the coffee, Mrs. DeMartini. And thank you for thinking of me right now. I need it."

If she only knew how much.

"Take care of yourself, Miss Lauren. And please stop by again to say hello. I've missed seeing you."

Lauren smiled and walked out onto the sidewalk.

Time to get down to business.

Chapter 26 – Detective Harding

Lauren arrived at the police station right on time and was pleasantly surprised when an officer quickly escorted her to Detective Harding's desk instead of having her wait in the general reception area. Lauren assumed it was because the news surrounding Collin's death, the investigation and her subsequent appearance in the newspapers made her a well-known face around the station.

Detective Harding stood as she approached.

"Ms. Brown, good morning," he said as he extended his arm and shook her hand warmly.

"Good morning, Detective. I'm sorry to jump start your morning unannounced like this."

"No, you're fine. How are you doing? I understand the funeral will be tomorrow, the 18th, correct?"

"Yes, that's right. In White Plains, his hometown."

"Ok, my condolences to his family and yours, of course."

Lauren smiled at him. Although there was no way to know what was going to happen when he interviewed her immediately after Collin's death, his friendly demeanor told Lauren that she had been eliminated as a suspect.

"Please sit."

"Thank you."

Detective Harding leaned forward in his chair and picked up his coffee mug. "So, what can I do for you, Ms. Brown?"

"Well, I am hoping you can tell me where I can find Jonathan Michael Jones."

Detective Harding practically choked on his coffee.

"Wha..."

Catching himself mid-swallow, he quickly grabbed a tissue from a desk drawer and wiped his chin.

"Sorry."

Lauren sat in silence.

"What did you say?"

"I am hoping you can tell me where to find Jonathan Michael Jones."

"How do you know who he is?"

"I just do."

Detective Harding gave Lauren a long, serious look and then sat back in his chair. Finally, he spoke.

"I'm keeping eyes on him."

"Because he's your prime suspect."

Detective Harding let out a long exhale. "I cannot discuss the details of this investigation with you, Ms. Brown. But no matter what, Jones is not just some regular Joe on the street. He's been in trouble in the past and he might be dangerous."

"Yeah, I'd say so. He murdered Collin."

"*If* he murdered Collin," Detective Harding corrected her.

"Yes. *If.*"

"What in the world do you want with him?" Detective Harding asked and then took another sip of coffee.

"I want to ask him some questions and *you* might be interested in what he has to say. Can you help me find him?"

"Like I already said, I'm keeping eyes on him. But no, I'm afraid I'm not telling you where to find him or anything else about him, for that matter. To do so could put you in danger."

Lauren sat in silence and looked at Detective Harding for a few seconds.

Ok. He won't help.

She smiled and stood up.

"Ok, Detective Harding. Thank you for your time."

"You're very welcome, Ms. Brown. If anything new comes to light, we will keep you informed."

He shook her hand and then added, "I'll be thinking of you tomorrow."

Lauren smiled and left his office.

He said I'm keeping eyes on Jones. Not WE'RE. That implies he's the one tailing Jones. So, I will tail him.

Lauren walked out of the station and got into her car, keeping an eye on who came in, or out, of the station.

Now I wait.

Chapter 27 - Stakeout

The rest of the morning went by quickly for Lauren. Satellite radio and scrolling through social media on her phone kept her entertained. Thankfully, by noon things got interesting.

"Here we go," Lauren said out loud as she watched Detective Harding exit the building, get into a car, and back out of the parking space.

She had seen enough police shows over the years to know better than to follow him too closely, but in a city this big, it was harder than it looked. Lauren found herself speeding up, then slowing down, running yellow lights and barely keeping her driving legal as she struggled to keep the right distance from Detective Harding's car. She was glad when he eventually pulled into the parking lot of Clark Street Liquors and turned off the engine. She found a space in the last row of cars and luckily it had a decent line of sight to him.

Ok, what are we up to now? she thought to herself.

Detective Harding stayed in his car and seemed to be watching the front door. As it turned out, he wasn't watching the store at all. Within ten minutes, a man came out of an apartment in a two-story building next door and bounded down the stairs toward the parking lot.

Jones!

He headed toward the last row. Straight. Toward. Her. Car.

Oh shit! Lauren panicked. *Do I start the car? No, he'll look at me for sure. And Detective Harding will too.*

She took the only available option - she tried to hide. Lauren threw herself down across the armrest and face-planted into the passenger seat. Holding her breath, she listened for Jones to open a car door and prayed it would not be hers.

A few moments later, Lauren heard a car start and begin to drive out of a parking spot. Raising her head slowly out of the seat, she peeked out over the dashboard. It was a black 4-door Toyota. And Jones was driving.

She shot a quick glance toward Detective Harding's car. Just then he started his engine and moved toward the parking lot exit, traveling in the same direction as Jones.

"Thank you, God," Lauren laid her head back into the driver's headrest and shut her eyes. "Thank you."

It was a few minutes before Lauren's heartbeat returned to a somewhat normal rate. She pulled the car out of the parking lot and turned toward home.

Now I know where to find him.

Chapter 28 - The Truth

Lauren woke on December 16th and immediately got to work on her plans for the day. Grabbing some food and water for the car, she headed to a local branch of her bank to withdraw cash. A lot of cash. If things went according to plan, she was going to need it. By 9:00am, she had pulled into the same parking space near Jones' apartment building and turned off the engine.

This is it. No matter what it takes, I'm going to talk to him today.

She was lucky. It didn't take long for Jones to appear outside his apartment and head down the stairs, toward his car.

Lauren took a deep breath and opened her car door. She stepped outside and walked toward Jones, meeting him beside his car.

"Jonathan Jones?" she asked.

"Who are you?"

"I'm someone who'd like to talk to you for a while. You in a hurry?"

Jones smiled and tilted his head to the side, running his eyes up and down over Lauren's body. "You wanna go somewhere?"

"Ahhhhhh, no. Here's fine."

"Well then, yeah, I'm busy."

Jones appeared disappointed there wasn't more being offered than a conversation.

"Ok. Listen. I can pay you for your time. Does that help free up your schedule?"

"Hey, lady, sure. You payin, I'm talkin."

Great. This I can work with.

She reached into her jacket and handed Jones $200.

"It's going to take more than that, honey."

Another $200 exchanged hands. Jones smiled.

"Shoot."

"First, I want to see if you know this man," Lauren asked as she opened her phone to a picture of Cam and held it up for Jones to see.

He nodded.

"He's my lawyer. Damn good one too. Got me outta a lot of shitty charges."

"Ok. Next question."

She handed him another $400.

"Do you know him?" she asked as she pulled up a picture of Theo and again, held up the phone to show him."

Jones replied quickly.

"Nope."

"Really? That was fast. You sure you don't wanna take a longer look at him?"

"Nope," Jones repeated. "Look, lady, I know lots of people. This part of town, they come and go, and they pretty much all look the same after a while."

Lauren stood quiet for a moment. Jones eventually broke the silence.

The Stall

"Ok, I'm outta here," Jones said and reached for the car door.

"Wait."

Lauren pulled out another $400 and held up the phone again.

"Look harder this time."

Surprisingly, Jones did as she asked. He bent toward the phone screen and studied Theo's face. When he stood back up, he sighed.

"Yeah, I know him. He paid me for a job," Jones chuckled. "And now you're payin me to talk about him. My lucky day, I guess."

Lauren paused and looked at the photo of Theo. She knew what she had to ask. This had been her plan all along. But now, she was almost afraid to hear the answer.

"What did this man ask you to do?"

Jones shook his head.

"No, not gonna talk about that. It's in the past. If you wanna know, you go ask him. I don't know who he is. He found me, he paid me."

Lauren took a deep breath and handed him $1000. Then she changed the photo on her phone to Collin. She held it up to Jones.

"He paid you to kill this man, didn't he?"

Jones took a long time to reply. Then suddenly, it was almost as if the pistons in his head were finally firing on all cylinders. His eyes got really large and he stared at Lauren.

"Wait a second. No *wonder* you're here throwing around all your cash! You're that rich New Jersey girl from the newspapers. You got a big inheritance when your parents died. And now you're some dead man's girlfriend. It was all over the news this month."

"So you *do* know who this is?"

Lauren held the picture of Collin back up to Jones' face.

"No, I don't know his name."

Lauren was getting more and more frustrated as the minutes went by. She had to change tactics.

"His name was Collin. And yeah, I was his girlfriend, the one from the papers."

Jones stood silently looking at Lauren.

"Let me jog your memory. George's bar over in Chelsea. Nice place and a little more upscale than this neck of the woods. You followed Collin out of the bar and into an alley."

Jones crossed his arms and stood silent. Defiant.

Lauren changed the picture back to Theo.

"Did this man ask you to do something to Collin? Please tell me."

Jones uncrossed his arms and stuck his hands in his pockets.

"Yeah. He said he'd pay me to scare him."

He paused.

"And if it got more serious, I'd get more. He didn't care what I did to him. That's all I'm gonna say. I got paid. It was just a job."

Lauren stood silently in shock. There it was. The truth.

"How much?" Lauren whispered.

"What?"

"How much did he pay you."

"Three grand."

Lauren handed Jones $800.

"There you go, Jones. That's all I got. Lucky you. You just made another three grand."

She walked away without saying another word.

Chapter 29 - Short and Sweet

Lauren's phone was blowing up the morning of December 15th. Abbie could not believe she wanted to come to work. It was to be the first shift since Collin was killed and her manager had actually taken her off the schedule. But once Lauren learned of that, she insisted on coming in. Little did they know, it was going to be the shortest shift in the history of the company.

When Lauren arrived, she insisted on working the counter. No one was going to argue with her, so Abbie and the others rearranged their assignments. It didn't take long for things to fall into place. Right on cue, Theo walked in.

"Good morning, sir. Can I take your order?" Lauren asked with a sweet, professional tone.

"Hello, yes, thanks. Grande, medium roast, black. Please."

"What's the name on this order?"

"Theo."

Lauren rang up the order and took Theo's money. Then she reached for the correct size of paper cup and a marker. She smiled as wrote on it.

"I'll go ahead and grab that for you now. You can wait here."

A few moments later, she placed the full cup of coffee on the counter.

"Here you are, sir. Have a great day."

"Thank you!" he replied as he picked up the coffee and turned to walk toward a seat at a table nearby.

He was only seated a few seconds before he abruptly stood up and quickly scanned the café for her face. But she was already out the door and down the block.

He slowly sat back down and stared at what Lauren had written on the cup:

Theo Briggs. I know what you did.

Chapter 30 - Reality

Lauren spent December 14th in her apartment, hiding from the outside world. It didn't really matter that the city was being hit with a huge snowstorm. She wouldn't have left anyway. The local shops were full of newspapers with headlines about Collin's death and photos from Lauren's family tragedy. Lauren would have to live without Mrs. DeMartini's fresh coffee. And going to see Parker and Steph was out of the question. They were undoubtedly dealing with the press over in New Jersey as well and Lauren wanted to be close to home in case Detective Harding asked her to come in to make a statement. She wasn't sure when that would happen, but it would be soon.

So instead, Lauren stayed inside and over the course of the day, and a bottle of wine, processed the unbearable truths she now knew and asked herself a lot of hard questions.

I've been living - and sleeping - with the man who plotted and paid for Collin to be killed. But I never fell in love with Theo. It was an agreement I made with myself. If I was going to get back to December and figure out the truth, I had to play along.

Accepting that fact, Lauren forgave herself.

Did I really NEVER suspect him? Never see any signs? Was he THAT clever? Lauren sat and thought about it.

No. I never suspected him. He never acted revengeful, angry, or even unkind, to anyone. He didn't hold grudges. He hardly even talked about the past.

But then a thought flashed in her mind. Had Theo *ever* spoken Collin's name? Her mind raced.

Think! Think!

Only once. Only once in six months had Theo said Collin's name out loud. It was when he questioned her about showing up at Collin's parents' house in White Plains. That was in May. And he told her to "let that go."

Theo didn't want to acknowledge that Collin ever existed or acknowledge the trauma of his death. Never wanted me to even think about him. On the outside, he looked like a boyfriend wanting to shield me from painful memories of the past. To spoil me. To make me happy. But maybe he was afraid I'd eventually dig into what happened.

Lauren sighed. While she played house, she hadn't noticed Theo ignoring the fact Collin ever existed.

Why did Theo do it? Why would this seemingly kind, smart, perfect man pursue me? For money? He never asked me for anything. I never paid for even a single meal over all those months.

The 'why' truly stumped Lauren.

Maybe it would have happened later. Maybe he would have proposed. And by then, would I have insisted on a pre-nup?

That thought made her cringe and the truth had been too much today. She crawled into bed, pulled the blanket up over her head, and yawned. Eventually, the wine, sirens and car horns lulled her to sleep.

Chapter 31 - Plans

Lauren woke on December 13th and laid in bed for quite a while, listening to the city come to life outside her window.

It's the 13th. Collin will be alive in 3 days.

Tears rolled down her cheeks.

I'm almost there.

But 'there' was a giant leap from where she was. There were a lot of things she had to figure out. Her mind started to organize the next three days.

How do I handle my interview with Detective Harding? I know I won't walk in proclaiming Theo paid Jones to kill Collin. He'd laugh me out of the building. I have to ignore that fact and give him what he expects - where I was and when I went home on December 10th.

Lauren picked up her phone and made sure the ringer was on.

He should be calling me today.

Putting her phone down, she moved on to the bigger question.

Am I going to stop Jones from killing Collin?

Lauren sighed.

What kind of woman would I be if I didn't?

Lauren put her head in her hands.

Logistically, it would be almost impossible to keep Collin alive at 2:00am on the 11th. I'm not going to be in George's when he leaves, so I can't just appear out of thin air and then magically keep him from walking toward the alley.

The weight of that revelation tore at Lauren's heart.

The only way to save him is to let the 11th happen. And then get back to the 10th. If I can do that, and we go to George's that night, I can get myself into that bathroom stall. Then maybe I can figure out how to get time moving forward again and keep Collin alive. That's what I need to do.

Buzz. Her phone rang.

Detective Harding.

She was wrong. Unknown number.

"Hello?"

"Is this Lauren Brown?" a woman asked.

"Yes. Who is this?"

"Lauren, my name is Sandra Kennedy. I'm a reporter for the Daily Note here in the city."

Lauren recognized the name immediately.

"Ok. What is this about?"

"I'm reporting on the events of December 11th and I was wondering if you would like to be quoted in the story."

Lauren thought back to Sandra's story that she had read online months earlier. She remembered that Sandra's writing seemed fair and factual, but still, Lauren was not sure being quoted in any press would be a good idea.

"I'm afraid not. Things are, well, too new right now. I'm not up for it."

"I completely understand. But before I let you go, I'd also like to find out more about your family in Summit. You lost your parents at a very young age, correct?"

Click. Lauren hung up on her.

Unbelievable. She didn't even miss a beat. She wasn't able to get something out of me about Collin, so she'd be happy to write about my parents. Note to self. Stop answering unknown calls.

As it turned out, Detective Harding did not call Lauren that day. But a lot of other people did.

Around 4:00pm, Parker called but left no message. A few minutes later, he texted.

Parker: *When can we come see you?*
Lauren: *I will let you know later. Love you.*

Abbie called, but Lauren let it go to voicemail. When Lauren listened it to later, Abbie was sobbing.

"Oh, Lauren, please call me back. Please let me come over."

Lauren did not call her back. Instead, she kept the outside world at arms' length and walked around the apartment with a glass of wine, thinking about Collin.

Remembering what Collin smelled like was easy. She stood in front of his closet and pulled one of his fleece jackets toward her. Shutting her eyes, she held it to her face and took a deep inward breath.

Oh, Collin. I'll see you in this really soon, sweetheart.

Then she tried to remember what his voice sounded like.

Wait! His voice!

Lauren quickly opened up her phone to her Favorites. He was there! Her hand shook as she hit 'Call'.

Ring. Ring. Ring. Ring.

"Hello, this is Collin. Sorry I missed you. I'm probably out doing something very exciting in the Big Apple, you know. Well, leave me a message and I'll call you back."

Beep.

Click.

By the time Lauren fell asleep that night, she had dialed that number 20 more times, just listening to his voice. And the phone, sealed away in an evidence bag somewhere in Detective Harding's station, showed all her missed calls.

Chapter 32 – The Interview

Lauren had hoped she would not have to wait long for Detective Harding to contact her about an interview. When he called her at 10:00am on December 12th, she was more than ready.

"Hello?"

"Hello, Ms. Brown. This is Detective Harding. We spoke yesterday morning when I came to your apartment."

Ok, so that's how I find out Collin is dead. He'll come to the apartment.

"Yes, hello."

"I was wondering if you would be able to come down to the station today so that we could take your official statement. It's routine, of course."

"Yes, I can come down."

"Ok, I can send a car to get you. What time is best?"

"I can come now, and I'll drive."

"It's really no problem to send a car. We don't want you driving when you've just had such shocking news."

Lauren thought about this. *Probably a good idea. No need to insist on driving myself.*

"You're right. Ok, I can be ready anytime."

"Great, I will send a car to collect you at 11:30am. Thank you, Ms. Brown. See you soon."

Right on time, Lauren saw a police car pull up in front of her apartment building. Walking out the front door, the officer got out of the car and greeted her.

"Ms. Brown?"

"Yes."

"Here you go," the officer replied and opened the back passenger door for Lauren.

The ride to the station was relatively quick, for city traffic, and conversation was light. Lauren made sure to speak only when spoken to, although normally she would have struck up a conversation about this being her first time in the back of a police car. Or asked about how long the officer had been on the force.

Grieving, Lauren. You're grieving.

She wasn't exactly faking it, but she'd been preparing for this day a long time. The wounds from Collin's death were months old, not hours.

When they arrived at the station, Lauren waited for the officer to open the door for her and he escorted her inside and took her to a small interview room. It was a good thing she was following him, as her instinct would have been to walk directly to Detective Harding's desk. A desk that, from their perspective, she had not been to yet.

Geez. Don't blow it.

The Stall

The officer asked her to take a seat and told her that Detective Harding would not be long. He was right. Detective Harding walked in before the door had even closed.

"Ms. Brown. Thank you for coming in so quickly. I cannot imagine how difficult the past day has been for you."

Try five months.

"Thank you, Detective. It's been very hard. I'm still processing it all."

"Of course you are. And that's why we appreciate you coming in today. It's important for us to hear from you."

Lauren smiled and sat demurely in her chair, waiting for him to speak again.

"Now, Ms. Brown, first of all, can you please switch off your phone while we talk? Less distractions."

Lauren did as he asked.

"Thank you. Now, can you please recall for me everything that happened when you and Collin were out on the night of December 10th."

Ok, brave girl. Here you go.

"Yes. Collin and I went to George's that night to discuss our Christmas plans. You see, every year around this time there's a lot of discussion on whose family we are going to spend it with. Collin is from White Plains. That's where his mother, father, brother and his family live. We went there for a lot of holidays. My family is from Summit, New Jersey. It's just my brother, his wife and two daughters there now."

Lauren paused.

"I assume you know our parents passed away."

Detective Harding gave Lauren a sympathetic smile. "Yes, I'm aware. Please go on."

"So, we normally didn't make the trip to Summit for holidays. Collin and my brother didn't see eye to eye on a lot of things. It was just easier to go to his folks'."

"What didn't they see eye to eye about?"

Shit. This is not about Parker.

"I quit college and moved to Chelsea as soon as I turned 20. And I met Collin soon after. Parker, my brother, has blamed Collin for keeping me in Chelsea instead of moving back home to be closer to them."

"Is that true?"

"No, absolutely not. Summit is nice. Very nice. But after my parents' death, I wanted a clean start. I love it here."

"Ok. Anything else Parker and Collin argued about?"

"Parker thinks I'm wasting my artistic talent by working at Starbucks. Collin just wanted me to be happy. Making coffee makes me happy. I love the people I work with and the customers we see every day. It's like a little family there, I guess. But Parker thinks I should want to do something in photography. So he blamed Collin for me not pursuing that. But please understand, it was just two men not seeing eye to eye. They didn't, like, *hate* each other."

Detective Harding nodded and wrote some notes. "Ok, so you went to George's that night to discuss Christmas plans."

"Yes. And we did. We decided to go to White Plains."

Detective Harding nods again.

"I guess you could say I was disappointed. I had hoped to see my nieces in Summit at Christmas."

Lauren paused and looked down at her lap.

Speak the truth, just be careful.

The Stall

"That's what it's about, right? The magic of Christmas. Seeing them open gifts or making cookies together. They are only going to want me around for a few more years and then I'm just some aunt."

Get back to Collin.

"So, I was disappointed and I kept drinking. Collin has tried to help me cut back. But if it's a particularly bad day, or I'm frustrated about something, I have a hard time stopping. Anyway, I don't know what time it was, but all I remember is Collin walking me outside and putting me in a taxi. Next thing I knew, you were at my apartment to tell me he was dead."

Lauren felt tears in her eyes.

"For him not to come home with me, I must have said something really bad. I just don't know what it was."

Detective Harding handed Lauren a tissue from a box on the table.

"Thank you, Ms. Brown. This is very helpful to us. Just so you know, your recollection of drinking to excess, Collin taking you outside and then him coming back in the bar without you, matches the information we gathered from the staff at George's and the few customers we were able to identify and locate."

Detective Harding finished making some notes and then looked at Lauren.

"Did Collin have any enemies or people he didn't particularly get along with?"

"No, everyone loved Collin."

Detective Harding nodded.

"Financially, any problems?"

Lauren shook her head.

"Ms. Brown, can you please answer out loud?"

"Oh sorry. No, no financial problems. Collin had a good job and there was, of course, my inheritance that we used when necessary."

Detective Harding wrote some additional notes and then looked up at Lauren.

"I'm sorry to have to ask this, Ms. Brown, but how was your relationship with Collin?"

Ok. I knew this was coming.

Lauren looked at him straight in the eye.

"I loved Collin with my whole heart and soul. He was my *entire* life. We may have had a few arguments about stuff now and then. Stupid stuff. But nothing, ever more serious than that."

Lauren rubbed her temple and wiped tears from her eyes.

"I have no idea how to survive without him."

Detective Harding wrote a few short notes and then put down his pen.

"Ms. Brown, I am truly very sorry this happened. Please know that we are doing everything we possibly can to find out who killed Collin."

"Thank you, Detective."

"Two more things."

"Ok."

"Please do not contact Collin's family right now. We are having difficulty reaching them and they may or may not know about his death yet."

"Ok."

"And I suggest you not answer your phone unless it is a known number. The press are doing their best to sensationalize Collin's death."

"Yes, I am well aware."

"Ok. If they become a problem, you let me know."

Lauren nodded.

Detective Harding stood up and held out his hand.

"Thank you again, Ms. Brown, for coming in so promptly today. I will have an officer drive you home now."

Lauren shook his hand. "Thank you. I appreciate everything you are doing."

And with that, Lauren was escorted to a car outside and driven home.

Once behind closed doors, Lauren poured herself a glass of wine and sat on the sofa. She looked at her phone and remembered it had been turned off while she met with Detective Harding. She turned it back on and immediately saw ten missed calls and 4 text messages from Abbie.

Of course, she's probably just hearing about Collin on the news today.

At first, she had no intention of replying, but then realized Abbie might show up at her door.

If this had happened to her, I'd show up, too. It's only 1:00pm. This'll pass the time.

Over the course of the next hour, Lauren spoke to Abbie about what happened and answered questions the best she could. Her replies were short and she tried not to appear too evasive, but it still felt that way.

She knew she could only share what she had told Detective Harding, comments along the lines of: "We went to George's. I drank too much and Collin sent me home in a taxi. Then the police showed up to tell me about what happened. I just got back from making my statement at the station."

Abbie was beside herself, insisting she come over and stay with Lauren for a few nights.

"Abbie, it's ok. I really want to be alone right now. I promise I'll call you."

Eventually, Abbie accepted Lauren's wishes and told her she'd call or text every day.

As soon as Lauren hung up with Abbie, Parker and Steph called. Lauren decided to take the call. She was warmed up after talking to Abbie and was comfortable with the story - or the lie - whichever the situation called for.

"Hey, sis. How are you doing today?" Parker's sympathetic tone made it clear to Lauren that Parker and Steph already knew about Collin.

I must have spoken to them on the 11th after I got the news from the police.

"I'm doing ok. I just got home from making my statement at the police station."

"Ok. Listen, I wanted you to know that Collin's parents just called us. The police were at their home about an hour ago."

"Yeah, Detective Harding told me not to contact them yet. He said they were having trouble reaching them. I'm glad to hear that they did."

"Yes. They called us because they didn't want to bother you quite yet." Parker paused and took a deep breath. "Oh, Lauren, it was awful. They were pretty composed when I first answered but after a few words they were both crying on the phone. I've never heard a person make sounds like they were making."

Parker and Lauren both sat in silence for a few moments.

Steph spoke up. "Lauren, they asked us to let you know they're thinking of you, too. And they are heartbroken for you."

Lauren thought about the reaction she'd received at Collin's parents' house when she had arrived at their door. For them, the months since Collin's murder had passed. They'd tried to go on with their lives. And then she showed up and ripped that wound wide open. Lauren could still remember the sound of them crying behind the front door. Guilt washed over her.

I was selfish. Confused. Lost. I'm so sorry.

"Thanks for letting me know. I will contact them at some point. Just not sure when I can do that."

"Of course. No one expects anything from you," Parker replied.

Steph spoke up.

"Lauren, can Parker and I come over? We'd like to see you. Just need to get a sitter. We shouldn't bring the girls right now."

"Sure, but can we talk about a day and time later? I'm really tired."

"Of course."

"Ok, please give the girls a big hug from me. I love you."

"We love you too, Lauren. Bye."

They hung up.

Lauren was emotionally spent after the calls ended, but fortunately it did take up most of the afternoon. By 4:00pm, she was opening another bottle of wine.

Collin is going to die at 2:00am while I'm in bed asleep. And I'm not going to stop it. I am the worst person ever.

Chapter 33 - It Is Done

Thanks to the combined effects of the amount of wine she had consumed plus sheer mental exhaustion from speaking with Parker, Steph and Abbie, Lauren spent the entire night on her sofa. Although she never woke up, she was tormented by vivid dreams.

In one dream, Collin's mother received a phone call on an old-fashioned corded land line. She kept repeating, "Collin? Collin? We can't hear you, honey?" Suddenly, the cord disconnected from the wall unit and fell to the floor, blood flowing out of the loose end of the cord.

In another dream, Lauren and Collin walked out of George's together. As they turned and went toward the alley, Jones appeared in front of them. Lauren yelled, "Oh my God. This is the guy I told you about!" Collin looked at Jones. Jones looked at Collin. Then they both began to laugh. Collin pushed Lauren toward Jones and said, "$400 well spent." Collin turned around, got into a taxi and rode away. Jones looked at Lauren and said, "Hey, it's just a job." Then he moved toward her with a knife.

In her final dream, Lauren sat on the toilet in the bathroom stall at George's. She looked up and saw that the stall door was locked. At that moment, a woman in heels entered the bathroom and walked up to the

The Stall

stall door. She began to knock on the stall door. "Hello? Lauren?" she said.

"Do I know you?" Lauren replied. The woman laughed and continued to knock, this time harder and in a sing-song voice called out, "Are you there? I have something for you." Then the woman waved a full bottle of wine under the door for Lauren to see. Lauren reached for the bottle but she couldn't quite grasp it so she grabbed the latch to unlock the door. But it wouldn't move. It was stuck. The woman continued to knock. "Come on out. You can have this!" She knocked harder. And harder. And harder.

Just then, Lauren opened her eyes and heard the building's intercom system buzzing throughout the apartment. Her heart was pounding as she went over to the keypad.

Shit. Compose yourself.

"Hello?" she said into the speaker.

"Hello, is this Ms. Lauren Brown?"

"Yes."

"Ms. Brown, my name is Detective Harding with the police. And with me is Detective Stanwick. May we come up? We need to speak with you."

"Yes, ok. Come in," Lauren said as she buzzed them through.

Here we go. I've been expecting this conversation. Keep calm.

It only took a few moments for Detective Harding and a female detective to appear at her door. They each showed Lauren their badge and reintroduced themselves.

"Ms. Brown, I'm Detective Harding and this is Detective Stanwick."

The female detective smiled and nodded at Lauren.

"May we please come in?" Detective Harding asked.

"Yes, sure." Lauren answered. As she turned to let them in, she motioned to the sofa she'd just slept on.

"Please sit..."

Shit. The bottles.

Two empty wine bottles sat on the coffee table. And one glass. Lauren quickly picked up the evidence of her night and put it in the kitchen.

"Please sit down," Lauren repeated.

"Thank you," the female detective replied as they both sat down.

Lauren reached for a chair and pulled it closer to the sofa.

"Ms. Brown, I believe you know a Mr. Collin James Hunt. Born the second of August 1997. Is that correct?"

"Yes. He's my boyfriend. Why? Has something happened?"

So far, so good.

"I'm afraid we have bad news. Mr. Hunt was found dead last night."

Lauren wasn't prepared for what came next. All of a sudden, Lauren began to cry - and it wasn't the practiced, prepared emotional response she had planned to give. That simple statement of Collin's death hit her hard.

She had known it was true since June, but since that time, she'd been preoccupied with her 'life'. She had faked her way through a relationship with Theo. She had existed under the constant stress of living her life *in reverse*. And then she had figured out a plan to get back to December 10th when Collin was alive, in hopes of keeping him alive. The severity - the weight - of it all came crashing down on her.

Both detectives sat quietly while Lauren held her head in her hands, weeping. After a few moments, she looked up. She was a broken woman.

The Stall

Keep talking. Ask questions.

"What...what happened?"

"He was found stabbed in an alley near George's shortly after 2:00am this morning."

"We were at George's together."

"Yes, we understand that you left before midnight. Mr. Hunt stayed until closing time. That's when he left and walked toward the alley."

"Oh."

Yes, I left him.

"You said he was stabbed?"

"Yes. It appears he may have been in a fight. There was broken glass all around him. And he was stabbed twice in the stomach."

"And someone found him?"

Lauren sat quietly and cried while she listened to them answer.

"A member of the public saw him in the alley and called police. I'm sorry to say that Mr. Hunt was already deceased when emergency responders arrived. Earlier this morning we interviewed the staff from George's and they identified you as Mr. Hunt's girlfriend. They knew your name. That's how we located you."

Lauren nodded her head.

"Ms. Brown, we would like to ask you some questions but we know this is a lot to take in right now. Would you be willing to come to our station tomorrow for an official statement?"

Lauren nodded again, through more tears.

"Ok. I will call you tomorrow to make arrangements. And one last thing. You should expect to get some calls from the press. They are already starting to report on this online and it won't be long before they find out your name. I suggest you only answer calls from people you know."

"Ok. Thank you."

The detectives looked at each other and nodded. They stood up together.

"We'll show ourselves out, Ms. Brown. Again, we are very sorry for your loss."

Lauren didn't move nor acknowledge the detectives as the apartment door closed behind them. From the hall, they could hear her crying. It was a sound they knew far too well.

Chapter 34 - Notifications

Around noon that day, Lauren sat back down on her sofa and wrapped a blanket around herself. She picked up her phone and called Parker's cell.

I know I have to call him today. Best do it now.

"Hey sis!"

"Parker."

Lauren's tone of voice went right over Parker's head.

"You're calling to tell me you're not coming for Christmas, right? Can't say I'm surprised."

Silence.

"Lauren? You there?"

"Oh Parker," Lauren began to cry again. "Collin's dead."

"What?! Dead?! Wait. Sorry. Steph! Put the girls in the other room and get back here now!" Parker barked orders in the background.

Lauren waited until Parker spoke again.

"Ok. You're on speaker with us both. Ok. What did you say?"

"Collin is dead. The police found him in an alley near a bar we go to. He was stabbed early this morning," Lauren struggled to get the words out.

Lauren could hear them both gasp and then heard Steph crying.

"Oh, no. Oh my God," Steph said. "I'm gonna be sick."

Lauren could hear her walking quickly away from the phone.

"Lauren, I can't believe it. How did you find out?"

"The police were just here. They want me to come to the station tomorrow for a statement."

"Yeah, ok. Wait a second. Weren't you there too?"

"No, no. I had actually le...," Lauren couldn't finish the words. She struggled to compose herself.

"I left him. I...," Lauren paused. "I drank too much. The bar staff saw him take me outside and put me in a taxi. I have no idea how I drank so much that I couldn't stay there or that he didn't want me there with him. Oh, Parker. I feel like I killed him. I'm such a horrible person."

"Lauren. No. This is *not* your fault. No matter what the circumstances, you are *not* to blame for this. If you had stayed, you might have been there with him and be dead too!"

Lauren blew her nose into a tissue and tried to compose herself.

"Lauren, I'm back," Steph said. "Sorry. I was sick. Not sure what I missed, but it's ok. Oh, honey. Can we come to see you?"

"Yes, yes, we should come right now," Parker agreed.

"No, not today. I, I need some time. I'll be ok, I just need some time." *No visitors.*

"Ok. Please call us if you change your mind."

"I will. Oh, and Parker."

"Yes."

"The police advised me to not answer calls from anyone I don't know. They said the press is already reporting on Collin's death online. They might try and reach me and I guess they may try to get to you guys, too."

And the press will be all over our parents' story very soon.

"Ok, good idea."

"Ok. I love you," Lauren sniffed.

"We love you, too," Parker and Steph chimed in together.

"Bye."

"Bye."

Lauren hung up and fell over onto the sofa cushions. She put her arm over her puffy and sore eyes.

Oh, Collin.

The extreme emotional reaction she had experienced during Detective Harding's visit had shocked her.

I thought I was prepared for it.

Lauren moved her arm and opened her eyes, but she couldn't see much. The room was too blurry, so she rubbed her eyes with her knuckles. Eventually things came into focus and she saw the empty bottles of wine sitting on the kitchen counter. Almost immediately, her stomach lurched and fell and Lauren threw her hands over her mouth. A few steps later and she was on the floor of her bathroom, vomiting into the toilet. The room began to spin and then everything went dark.

Chapter 35 – Ramifications

Lauren opened her eyes to an up-close and personal, full exposure view of her toilet base and bathroom tile.

"Ugh," Lauren said as she closed her eyes and rolled onto her back, avoiding any more of the grimy view from the floor.

Slowly, she sat up and then stood, steadying herself with one hand on the toilet's water tank. It didn't take long for her to realize she needed to flush. And that she needed a shower.

Thirty minutes later, she felt better. Not great. Not renewed. But at least able to put one foot in front of the other and feel something unfamiliar: Hunger.

How long has it been since I ate?

Lauren could not remember.

Ok, that's a problem.

She walked into the kitchen and opened the refrigerator. Lauren saw a fully stocked fridge. Vegetables, freshly marinated chicken, take-and-bake baguettes, fruit, bottled water, and more. Lauren smiled as she remembered Collin had been to the market earlier in the day on the 10th.

"Thank you, Collin."

The Stall

Lauren looked at her phone. 6:35pm.
Let's get started.

By 7:25pm, she was sitting down at her kitchen counter with a beautiful meal in front of her.
Ah!
Lauren jumped up. She had almost forgotten the wine. And then she stopped. She turned to the fridge and grabbed a bottle of sparkling water and a lime.
At 7:28pm, she was enjoying her dinner.
My last dinner alone. Collin will be here in a few hours.

Chapter 36 - Waiting

Even with a full stomach, there was plenty of room for butterflies that night. Lauren laughed at herself.

I feel like my boyfriend is coming over for the first time.

Having cleaned up after dinner, Lauren walked out of the kitchen at 8:15pm and decided the rest of the apartment was a mess. She started with the bathroom and then focused on the living room.

Better. Doesn't look like I slept here. How about the bedroom?

By 10:00pm, everything in Lauren's apartment was clean, picked up and looking great.

It isn't a homecoming, but it feels like it.

Between the butterflies and the long, near comatose nap she'd had on the bathroom floor, there was no way Lauren was falling asleep before midnight. She replayed the logic in her head.

At midnight, it'll be Sunday, December 10th. We don't go to George's until dinnertime that night. So, Collin will be here, in the apartment, at midnight. In two hours.

The Stall

Lauren decided that the best place to wait was the sofa. Read a book. Watch tv. Do something normal.

The longest two hours...ever.

Chapter 37 - Reunion

"Hey. Why are you still awake?"

The six most beautiful words in the English language were heard right at midnight, coming from the bedroom. Lauren practically choked on her tears attempting to speak.

"Hey," Collin repeated and stuck his head out the bedroom door.

Lauren turned to look at him and broke down on the sofa.

"Collin."

He walked over and sat down, his arms reaching around and enveloping her in a strong, tight hug. Lauren still couldn't speak. She was shaking.

"Hey, what's wrong?" Collin asked as he pulled back and looked at Lauren, concerned.

Lauren took a deep breath. "I'm fine. Sorry."

She pointed to a stack of books on the side table. "Got sucked into a good book."

"Ok. But you look really shook up. You sure you feel ok?"

Lauren smiled through ugly tears. "Yes, 100% great."

Collin took her by the hand. "Let's get some sleep, OK?"

The Stall

Lauren nodded and followed him.

A few minutes later, Collin was curled up behind Lauren. She could feel his breath on the back of her neck and his arm across the top of hers. For a moment, a similar memory of Theo flashed in her mind but she brushed it away.

This is what familiar comfort feels like. This is love. And this I will protect.

Chapter 38 - Reunited

Lauren had fallen asleep quickly that night. Collin's weight and warmth lulled her to sleep easily. It was such a deep sleep, in fact, that when she woke up on December 10th, she had forgotten he was there. But it lasted just an instant. She was now fully awake and she laid quietly next to him for a few minutes, looking over every inch of his face and taking in deep breaths, enjoying his smell.

Man, I missed you.

She ran her hand over Collin's lips, nose, cheeks, forehead, and then began to play with the waves of his hair. It was eventually enough to wake him.

"Is this an examination?" Collin joked, peeking at her with one eye open.

"Yes, sir. It is."

"Am I the doctor or the patient?"

Lauren leaned in and began to run her hand under the sheet covering Collin's chest, slowly moving downward.

"You're definitely the patient."

The Stall

And with a small laugh, Lauren leaned in and kissed him. It was close to noon before either of them came out of the bedroom.

"I think we're getting low on coffee," Collin called out from the kitchen. "Can I just run down to Mrs. DeMartini's and grab us two?"

"Sure, sounds good," Lauren yelled back from the bathroom.

"K. Be back soon."

Collin pulled a sweater on over his head and went out into the hall.

Lauren heard him lock the door from the outside and she noticed his absence right away. The apartment was eerily quiet. It had only been 12 hours, but she had already grown used to having Collin there. Home.

After all those months of truly being on my own, I get him back for 12 hours and I miss him when he leaves for coffee.

She let out a small laugh.

Then suddenly, the stillness in the air was unsettling and another feeling set in. Fear.

What if something happens to him again? What if he runs into Jones and I'm not there to recognize him? What if he gets hit by a car?

Lauren's mind was racing with worst-case scenarios. She had to stop herself.

Breathe. This is just PTSD, residual anxiety, whatever it is.

She tried to tell herself to be logical. But it didn't work. 20 seconds later she grabbed her jacket and ran out the door.

"Collin! Wait!"

She caught up to him halfway down the block. She was winded and had to stop to catch her breath.

"Whoo! Sorry! Just decided to get some fresh air with you."

"You're funny. Ok, come on. I need caffeine," he said as he took her by the arm and they walked together toward the shop.

Lauren was actually pleased she had dashed out and joined Collin. Cups of coffee in hand and their arms entwined, she suggested they take the long way home and it ended up being a really nice trip around the neighborhood. They were both in a good mood, no doubt brought on from their time together that morning plus the sunshine and the unusually mild December air. Lauren decided this might be the right time to start a conversation about Christmas - one that, if it went to plan, they'd finish at George's about 6 hours later.

"Hey, I've got something to ask you about," Lauren said, leaning into Collin's arm and giving it an extra squeeze.

"Oh boy. What now?" Collin replied, half joking.

"Come on. Be nice."

"Ok, I'm ready."

Lauren took a deep breath. "So, I wanted to talk about Christmas plans. And before you say anything, I feel very strongly about going to see my brother and family."

Collin stayed silent for a few moments.

He's either going to blow up at me or give me the silent treatment. I don't expect any other reaction.

Collin didn't say anything but kept his arm around Lauren's as they walked. Lauren was getting antsy.

"Well?"

"You said not to say anything."

"I'm done. You may speak now," Lauren laughed.

The Stall

"Ok. I hear you. But you know how I feel about Parker. So why insist we go *this* year?"

"Because of that very reason. We never go."

Lauren took another deep breath.

"Thing is, I miss my brother. Steph and I get along great. And then there's the girls. They are growing up super-fast and right now, at least, I'm still the cool-aunt."

Lauren stopped and turned to look at Collin.

"I know this is not your preference, but can we please agree to go to Summit this year? Do it for me."

Collin nodded.

"Ok. I'll agree. But please know that this whole thing with Parker is more on him than on me. He's the one who has been so critical of us both and our choices."

"I hear you. And I am going to speak to him. Any disrespect he shows toward you is disrespectful to me, too."

Collin nodded his head again and then turned to keep walking.

"Hey," Lauren stopped him. "Thank you."

She leaned in and gave him a kiss.

"You're welcome."

They walked on for about ten steps and then Collin stopped abruptly.

"Shit. How do we know what kind of presents the girls would like? We buy the wrong thing and Parker will just criticize it."

Lauren gave him a huge hug. "Oh, babe. I love you. Don't worry, I know EXACTLY what to get them!"

Lauren smiled to herself as they walked toward home.

I'll just buy what I bought before!

Lauren didn't even wait to get home to call Parker and Steph with the news.

"Hey sis, what's up?" Parker said as he answered.

Lauren could tell Parker was in a good mood.

"Well, just calling to see if there would be room for two more people at your house for Christmas this year! Collin and I would love to join you guys!"

"Really? Well, yeah, yeah, sure! Hey, Steph! Collin and Lauren are coming for Christmas!"

He sounded genuinely happy.

Lauren looked at Collin with the biggest grin on her face and gave him a big thumbs-up sign. Collin smiled and winked at her.

Mission accomplished!

Chapter 39 – George's

Lauren was so pleased with how the Christmas conversation had gone that she had completely forgotten about going to George's. Luckily, Collin brought up dinner plans at 5:30pm.

"Hey, so I've got some marinated chicken in the fridge. Sound ok for dinner?"

Shit!

Lauren looked at her phone and noticed the time.

Oh, thank God. Plenty of time.

"Hey, I had a thought. How about we go to George's. I've been craving their burgers and I think that's the special tonight."

Come on, Collin. Say yes.

Collin shut the fridge door.

"Ok, sounds good. But we should do the chicken tomorrow for sure."

"Great! Let's go now before it gets busier. I'm starving anyway."

Lauren grabbed their jackets and they walked out together.

It was a short walk from the apartment to the bar, and normally, Lauren was happy with that. But tonight, she would have preferred it be a bit longer. In her joy of having Collin home and her plans for Christmas all set, Lauren had not mentally prepared herself for the events that would occur tonight. But at this point, there was nothing she could do.

Let's go.

She took a deep breath and walked into Geoge's ahead of Collin.

"Hey Collin. Hey Lauren."

Almost all the staff in George's knew them by name.

"The usual?"

"Yeah, thanks," Collin replied and headed to an empty table.

"Um, actually, can I do a club soda and lime for me? Plenty of ice, please."

Collin looked at her but didn't say anything. After a few minutes, the waitress brought over Collin's beer and Lauren's water.

"Here you go, guys. Menus tonight?"

"Yes, thanks."

The waitress left and came back with two menus and silverware.

"You two probably already know this but burgers are on special tonight. Buy one get one half off. Unlimited toppings. And we've got sweet potato fries if you prefer. Or the normal fries. You need some more time?"

Collin handed her the menu. "Nope, I know what I'm having."

Lauren smiled. "Yeah. Me too."

They ordered the same thing. Burgers, medium well, American cheese, sliced tomato and pickle. Sweet potato fries and plenty of mayo on the side.

"Easy. Got it. Thanks," the waitress replied and walked away.

Collin picked up his beer and held it up.

"Here's to our future."

Luckily, Lauren hadn't taken a drink yet or else she may have spit it out.

Sounds familiar.

"Here's to us," she answered and they clinked their glasses together.

Collin took a long drink of beer and sat his glass back down. Then he cleared his throat so loudly that it made Lauren wonder if there was a problem.

"So. I couldn't help but notice you didn't order wine. Everything ok?"

"Yeah, just didn't feel like drinking. Maybe later."

"Oh!" Collin replied quickly and sat back abruptly in his seat. "Ok. That's good. I mean, I've been sitting here wondering if you were pregnant."

He let out a nervous laugh. Lauren wasn't sure how to take that.

"No, I'm not pregnant. It's just that, well, I've decided that I've been drinking too much lately. I guess I realized I've been using it as a reward for a good day, and a reward for a bad day, and a reward for getting through pretty much everything else in between. So, I'm cutting back. Nothing drastic. Just cutting back."

Collin nodded and stayed silent.

"And by the way, would it be the worst thing in the world if I were? Pregnant?"

"No, no, not at all. Honey, that would be great and I'd be very happy!" Collin reached over and squeezed Lauren's hand. "It's just that when, er I mean, if, it happens, please tell me. Don't do it subtly like stop drinking all of a sudden."

"Deal."

Lauren held up her glass to clink with Collin's again. They both took a long drink.

"So, I take it Parker and Steph are happy we're coming for Christmas? We'll just drive there on Christmas Day, right?"

"Yup. They were thrilled. Maybe you couldn't hear, but when Parker yelled over to Steph to tell her, she let out a little 'whoop whoop'. I'm sure they told the girls as soon as we hung up."

Collin smiled. "Ok, we can drive over on Christmas morning closer to lunchtime. Give them time to open gifts as a family."

"Perfect. And you know, we could drive up to White Plains on New Years Eve. Maybe we should see if everyone would be around and want us to come up?"

Collin's face lit up.

"Yeah, you're right. That might actually work. I think Ben mentioned something about him hosting a New Years Eve party for some friends up there. Maybe Mom and Dad would come over to Ben's house earlier in the day and we could see them too. I'll call Ben tomorrow."

Lauren smiled.

Barista and family negotiator. All in one.

Dinner arrived a few minutes later and everything was perfect. They ate in almost complete silence except for the sound coming from the TVs on the wall and the other customers seated around them. It was about 15 minutes into their meal when Lauren needed to use the bathroom.

No. I'm not ready yet.

She held it.

Five minutes later, there was no 'holding it' any longer.

The Stall

Ok brave girl. Time to go. Literally.

Lauren got up from her chair slowly. "I'm going to the bathroom. If she comes by, can you grab me another club soda and some extra limes this time?"

She kept her hand on Collin's shoulder the entire time.

"Ok, sure."

Lauren stayed next to Collin a few extra seconds.

"I love you, Collin."

"Yeah, me too," Collin replied, only half listening and totally engrossed in the TV coverage of that night's football game.

Lauren turned and walked toward the ladies' room door.

Chapter 40 - The Stall

The ladies' room was empty as Lauren walked in and headed to the second stall. Unbuckling her jeans and turning around, she sat down and let out a sigh.

What was I thinking about that night?

Then it came back to her. She had moved to Chelsea after dropping out of school, had an amazing apartment, a nice job at Starbucks, Collin, and not much else to worry about.

I think the past six months have given me plenty to worry about.

A few moments later, the door to the ladies' room opened and Lauren heard the click of high heels walk toward the stalls.

Here we go.

Lauren looked up to see the latch on the door. Unlocked. She held her hand against the door, not shutting it but just keeping it in place. The woman walked up and stood in front of Lauren's stall door. The tips of her black heels were just visible under the stall door.

Just like Mom's.

Lauren felt the door move against her hand. Lauren spoke first.

"This has to stop."

The Stall

The pressure of the door on Lauren's hand released.

"What did you say?" the woman asked.

"The past six months. Time moving backwards. I don't know why you chose me but it all started right here and now it has to stop. Please."

Lauren heard her own voice crack.

The woman stood silent for a few moments, then finally spoke.

"You said I chose you. The truth is you chose yourself. You're the one who needed me."

"That makes no sense."

"Think of me as someone who came to help when you needed it."

"Help? Because of you, my boyfriend was murdered and I lost months of my life! I've been living with a complete stranger!"

"True, but here you are. You figured out how to survive and get back here. To today. And you discovered the truth about what happened to Collin. You did all that on your own, Lauren."

Lauren sat in silence.

"So, Lauren, what have you learned?"

"What?"

"What have you learned? Through this entire process. What did you learn?"

Lauren closed her eyes and put one palm to her forehead. She took a deep breath.

"I learned not to take life for granted. I thought I had learned that when my parents died, but I was so young. I wasn't capable of understanding that lesson yet. Moving here, with Collin in my life and more than enough money to live on, things came easy. But after losing him and surviving, alone, the past six months, I know I took him for granted."

"Go on."

"And my brother and his family, too. Ever since moving here, I've allowed my life to go by without them in it. I never stood up and said they were important to me. That's on me. But the time I've spent with them since June, it's been amazing. So things will be different now."

"Go on."

Lauren opened her eyes and took more deep breaths.

"And I know that I'm drinking too much. In some messed up, indirect way, Collin paid the price for that and my body is telling me it's time to slow down."

"Sounds like you've learned a lot."

"Yeah. I guess I have."

"Lauren, are you ready for this to end now?"

"Yes. Please."

"Ok, it can stop but you know what has to happen next."

Lauren looked down at the floor and then very slowly released her hand from the door. In an instant, the door flew toward her and hit her directly in the top of the head.

Stars. Lights. And an incredibly sharp pain drilled into the top of Lauren's head. Lauren sat in silent pain while the woman walked quickly toward the bathroom door and left.

Lauren sat for a few moments, wiping the tears from her eyes and thinking about what just happened.

Am I done? Is this done?

The Stall

Gathering her strength, she stood up and walked out of the stall. She couldn't wait. She didn't even make it to the mirror. Looking down, she saw her boots and jeans. She was back.

Oh, thank God. It's over.

A few moments later, Lauren opened the door of the ladies' room and walked out. Collin was waiting for her, smiling.

"So, who's going to win tonight?" Lauren asked as she sat back down in her seat.

Collin replied, in great detail, with way more information than she really cared to know. One team's star tight end was out sick. The other team's defensive line was down to second string. And a kicker had a sore toe. Lauren listened. Nodded. Even smiled a few times at his funny comments. And all the while, she was taking in every inch of his face.

I'm never taking this for granted again.

By 9:30pm, dinner was over and it had started to get crowded in George's.

"Wanna head out soon?" Collin asked.

Lauren was glad to hear him say that. She'd been keeping an eye on the door the entire evening, wondering when Jones would arrive. So far, he had not.

Lauren glanced at her phone and nodded.

"Yeah. Let's go."

A few minutes later, they had paid the bill and grabbed their jackets to leave. Collin opened the door for Lauren to walk out, but she paused before going outside. She gave the bar one more glance, looking at faces.

He's not here.

She let out a sigh of relief and walked out. Lauren couldn't help but look over her shoulder every few steps during the walk home. It was so frequent that Collin eventually noticed.

"Hey," he said, looking behind himself as well, "are you looking for someone? You keep turning around."

"Sorry, nothing. Never mind."

But she didn't really relax until they had walked through their apartment door and locked it behind her.

"Movie tonight?" Collin asked as he took off his jacket.

"Don't you want to watch the game?"

"No, it's gonna be a landslide. A movie is fine with me."

"Perfect!"

After some back and forth, they settled on a new spy thriller. Lauren looked at the movie's length: 2 hours 30 minutes.

That'll take us past midnight. It'll be December 11th when the movie ends.

Lauren looked at her phone a few times over the course of the film, nervously waiting for 12:01am. The movie was so engrossing, however, that she completely forgot about the time until it had ended and Collin turned off the TV.

She looked down and saw:

The Stall

12:32am
Monday, December 11, 2023

Time is going forward. It's really over.

Chapter 41 – Line of Sight

Collin was up early for work that morning and so he left a note for Lauren on the kitchen table.

"Text me when you are up. We need some stuff from the store. Do you work today?"

Lauren opened the app on her phone to see her work schedule.

Nothing today. Good thing, because I've got someone to visit.

She texted Collin as she walked to the bathroom for a quick shower.

Lauren: *Good morning. No work today. Let me know the groceries you'd like me to pick up later. Love you.*

Within the hour, Lauren had withdrawn more cash at the bank and pulled into the liquor store parking lot. She quickly scanned the lot in hopes of seeing Jones' Toyota.

Bingo. Last row, same as before.

She parked in the same row, four spots down and switched off the engine.

The Stall

Time to get comfortable.

Lauren spent the next hour going over what she planned to say to Jones. She'd need him to confess his unsuccessful plan to kill Collin and how Theo had paid him to do it. And she'd need to record it. It was a long shot, but if she was going to tell the police that Theo had been, and was still, a threat, she needed proof.

She grabbed her phone and pulled up a photo of Theo online. Luckily, Anderson, Thomas and Cooper's firm had headshots of all their partners and junior partners on their website. Looking at Theo's smiling face made her stomach turn. She took a screen shot of it to show Jones later. A few moments later, Collin texted her his grocery list. Lauren smiled.

It was just then that something caught her attention out of the corner of her eye. A car entered the parking lot.

A black Audi S8.

Theo?

Lauren couldn't believe her eyes. It *was* Theo. She'd recognize that car anywhere and she even caught a glimpse of his face as he steered into a space in the first row of the parking lot, two rows in front of her. There he sat, car idling, directly in her line of sight to Jones' apartment building.

"What are *you* doing here?" she asked herself out loud.

Lauren quickly opened her phone's Camera app and started a video. She had barely focused the camera on the Audi's license plate when she looked up and saw Jones come down the stairs of his apartment building. Walking straight toward Theo. Theo unrolled his window.

Holy shit.

Lauren struggled to hear their exchange through the glass of her car windows, but she didn't need to hear *every* word to understand it perfectly. Jones' demeanor and the sheer volume of their conversation made it clear what was being said.

"...not there," said Jones.

"Why...not?" said Theo.

"...don't know."

"...go tonight...."

"...gonna cost..."

"No. We had a deal..."

"... more money..."

"Fuck you. We had..."

"Maybe I just need to forget..."

"NO! Go find him!"

"You're crazy. I'm out."

And with that, Jones turned away and started to walk directly behind Theo's Audi, heading for his car. Lauren's hands shook as she witnessed the horror of what came next.

Within seconds, Theo threw the car into reverse, striking Jones on the side of his body. The force of the Audi's back bumper bounced Jones directly into the front bumper of the car parked behind Theo. Looking back, Theo gunned his engine and continued in reverse, slamming the back of his Audi into Jones, now crushed between the cars. Jones never made a sound. Suddenly, Theo sped forward and steered toward the exit of the parking lot. He never looked back.

The Stall

Lauren sat in absolute shock at what had happened. She couldn't see Jones anymore, but she assumed his lifeless body laid crumpled on the ground. For what seemed like minutes, she sat stunned and uncertain of what to do. Just then Lauren realized she was still recording. She had captured it all. She quickly ended the video.

"Oh my God. Oh my God," Lauren repeated to herself as she sat in the car shaking uncontrollably.

Theo just killed Jones! I've got to call the police!

Just as she opened her Phone app, she paused.

If I call the police and tell them what I have on video, I have to explain WHY I was videoing Theo. And I'll be a witness to a murder. And that means court. Do I really want that?

Lauren thought through her options.

License plate. Anonymous. And not from my phone. That's the only way.

As Lauren started her car, she saw two men exit the liquor store. Luckily for her, they walked in the direction opposite of Jones' body. Lauren took a deep breath and pulled slowly out of the parking lot, toward the market.

Chapter 42 - Anonymous

Lauren memorized the phone number for Detective Harding's precinct as she walked up to the courtesy counter.

"Car trouble and my cell's dead. Can I use the phone?"

The teenage clerk didn't even glance up from her own phone but instead simply pointed to one sitting on the counter a few feet away. Lauren pulled the unit as far from the clerk as the cord would allow, then dialed quickly.

"May I speak with Harding, please," Lauren asked calmly, not adding the title "Detective" in case the teenager was actually listening. A few moments later, he answered.

"Detective Harding."

"I want to anonymously report a murder I witnessed about 20 minutes ago in the parking lot of Clark Street Liquors. A man named Theo Briggs was driving a black Audi S8 and he purposely hit another man with his car. The license plate is..."

Lauren spoke calmly and succinctly, trying not to draw attention to the fact she was reporting a murder while standing just a few feet away

The Stall

from the teenager. When she paused, Detective Harding repeated what she had said and asked if she was sure she did not want to give her name.

"No. Mr. Briggs is a very dangerous man. Good-bye."

Click.

That's the best I can do.

Lauren hung up and walked away. Once she was out of the clerk's sight, she pulled out her phone and read Collin's text with his grocery list. Closing that app, Lauren looked down at what was still open on her phone. Staring her in the face was the parking lot video - Jones' murder - right there in full color.

They'll find Theo soon enough. But with Cam on his side, he's not going away that easily. We are still in danger.

Chapter 43 – Time For A Change

Lauren had barely unpacked the groceries when Collin walked in from work.

"Hey," Lauren said as Collin walked through the apartment door.

"Hi. Thanks for picking up that stuff."

Collin gave a loud sigh as he sat at the kitchen island.

"I'm exhausted," he mumbled.

"No problem. I'll cook tonight. What do you want?"

"We need to eat the chicken, but I need carbs. Lots. You got the pasta, right?"

"Yup, and bread."

"Perfect."

I could use some comfort food too.

Forty-five minutes later they sat down to eat and Lauren couldn't wait any longer.

'Collin, there's something I want to discuss tonight."

"Sure, hon." Collin replied, as a forkful of penne and vodka sauce disappeared into his mouth.

The Stall

"I think we should move."

Collin practically choked.

His first reaction was shock. Hadn't she always loved Chelsea? They had a great neighborhood. George's was within walking distance. It was such a safe area. Her work was close. His reasons to stay put were valid.

After he was done, Lauren did her best to explain why she thought it was time to leave. Apartment life had been great, but she was tired of living with neighbors so close by. Plus, they had more than enough money to considering buying a house.

His second reaction was silence. But she wasn't surprised. She knew none of those reasons would affect Collin enough to get him to agree to move, right then and there. So, she played her last card.

"And remember how I was looking over my shoulder a lot when we left George's last night? I probably should have mentioned it before, but I've started to feel like someone is following me."

With Jones dead, it wasn't exactly the entire truth, but Theo was still a real threat. Luckily, she didn't need to say anything else.

"Ok," Collin said as he nodded his head and reached over to give her a long hug. "Ok. Let's go."

By the time dinner ended, they had a plan. Collin rang his parents to ask if he and Lauren could come visit for "a while." To say that his parents were thrilled was an understatement. They were so happy, they never asked why. Collin told them they'd pack up some items and be there within a day or two.

They spent the rest of the evening sitting together, looking at online real estate listings and sending inquiries to agents about open houses. And to Lauren's surprise – and delight - Collin even agreed to call Parker and Steph the next day to get their thoughts on good townships in New Jersey.

When Lauren went to bed that night, her mind was racing. Things had moved fast. So fast, in fact, that Lauren struggled with the idea that once again, Theo had taken control over her life.

Am I letting him dictate what I do? Where we live?

It wasn't a pleasant feeling.

But I've got to be realistic. Theo's a lawyer. He's smart. An until he's behind bars, there's a very good chance he could come looking for me - and Collin.

Lauren knew that was *very* possible. And it was that thought that finally put her mind at ease. By taking that threat seriously, *she* was the one in control.

We're moving forward. I'm moving on.

Chapter 44 - Moving On

The next morning, Collin and Lauren broke the news to their employers. Collin rang his boss and negotiated a work-from-home agreement. Next, Lauren called her manager and was surprised to hear that transfers between café locations were common and easy to accommodate. Lauren had a few shifts at the White Plains location scheduled to begin a week later.

Up next, it was time to tell Abbie, and she was shocked to hear Lauren would not be back to work. Lauren kept the reasons short and basic, mostly centered around being ready for home ownership. It was a sad goodbye but they promised to visit each other, "all the time."

The last order of business was to call Mr. Davis and give him their 30 days' notice.

"I'm sorry to hear you two are leaving us, Lauren," Mr. Davis said.

"Thank you for saying that, but it's time that Collin and I stretch our wings a bit, I guess."

"Of course. We will miss you!"

Their move-out date was settled easily. They agreed on a vacate date 30 days in the future.

"If you need to reach us for any reason, please email or call me. We may not be around the apartment much," Lauren added at the end of the call.

They said their final good-byes and hung up.

That tie is cut.

Or so she thought.

Chapter 45 - A Visitor

By the morning of Thursday, December 14th, Collin and Lauren had packed up the necessities in their apartment and started the drive north to White Plains. While Collin drove, Lauren opened her laptop and searched the city's arrest records. No Theo Briggs. The only thing she was able to find out was that, according to his firm's website, he was still employed there. His smiling headshot still present on their list of junior partners.

No way to tell if he's even been questioned. But I'm sure he will be.

It was just then that Lauren's laptop pinged. An email from Mr. Davis had arrived. Lauren's stomach jumped as she saw the subject line.

Visitor looking for you

Hello Lauren,

Yesterday, Mrs. Adams called me and asked if I knew where you were. She said her grandson had stopped by and wanted to see you. He had knocked on your door but you and Collin must have both been out. I told Mrs. Adams that I did not know where you were and that was the end of the conversation yesterday. Then this morning about 10 minutes ago, she rang me again and said her grandson was in her apartment and insistent that she call 'the landlord' to find out how to contact you. I immediately went to Mrs. Adam's apartment to talk to him. At first, he was very polite and said that you and he were old friends and that you had asked him to stop by when he was in the area. When I told him I had no intention of telling him anything about your whereabouts, he became very angry. At that point, I left Mrs. Adam's apartment and came home to email you right away.

I will keep an eye out for him and if he continues to loiter around the building, or contact me again, I will let you know. In the meantime, please call me before you or Collin return to the building so we can ensure he is not there at the same time.

Please take care. I do not get a good feeling about him.

Mr. Davis

Lauren's heart was pounding.

He hasn't been arrested. He's looking for me.

She quickly typed out a response.

Mr. Davis,

That man is Theo Briggs. He is very dangerous. If he continues to come around and ask where I am, pass on a message for me. Tell him, "She asked how your bumper was and that she has it on video."

Take care,

Lauren

More deep breaths. Lauren looked at Collin and reached over to run her fingers through his hair. Collin smiled back at her.

The Stall

I'm so glad we left when we did.

It wasn't long before Lauren was back online. She spent the next 20 minutes typing on her laptop.

"Everything ok?" Collin asked, looking over at her as he drove.

"Yup, just taking care of something I should have finished a long time ago."

"Secret?"

"For now. I'll tell you how it ends up," Lauren replied and winked at him.

Lauren refocused her mind on her laptop and continued to type. After ten more minutes, Collin spoke up.

"Hey, we're getting close to Mom and Dad's place."

Lauren shut the laptop.

"Ok. I'm done. Are you getting excited to see your folks?" Lauren asked.

"Yeah. And I'm sure Mom will be watching for us and be out on the driveway before we put it in park."

Lauren smiled and turned to look out the window, her fingers drumming across the top of her laptop. The uncertainty of what would happen with Theo, if anything, was unsettling but she knew she had to focus on the things she could control – her dreams, her future, with Collin, one day at a time. Moving forward.

Chapter 46 - Happiness

It was the happiest of holidays for Lauren and Collin. During a quick pre-Christmas call to her brother, Lauren asked Parker to *please* make every effort to get along with Collin. And she reminded Collin of the same thing during the drive to Summit. As it turned out, it worked. The only raised voices were the girls screaming in delight as they unwrapped their gifts.

"My gosh. Lauren and Collin, you've spoiled them."

Parker laughed as the girls ran off to play with their new toys.

Lauren smiled and thought that sounded familiar.

"Hey, they're only young once!"

Parker smiled and then did something very odd. He briskly rubbed the top of his head.

"You ok?" Lauren asked.

"Oh yeah, I'm fine. Just hit my head the other day."

Lauren stared at Parker for a long moment.

Probably nothing. Let it go.

The Stall

He finally spoke up.

"Now, tell me about your house hunting. Am I *actually* going to get my sister back in the state of New Jersey?" Parker asked with a teasing tone.

Lauren smiled and shrugged.

"Who knows. There might be some plans being made that'll bring me around here more often."

Parker smiled and looked at Collin.

"Beer?"

"Yes sir!" Collin replied.

Parker then turned toward Lauren.

"Hey, I picked up your favorite wine to have with lunch today. You ready for a glass?"

Lauren shook her head.

"No, I'm ok right now. But go ahead without me. I'm cutting back."

Parker shrugged and smiled.

"Ok, sis. Don't take this the wrong way, but I'm glad to hear that."

Lauren smiled and nodded.

Six days later, Lauren and Collin pulled up to Ben and Angela's house for their New Year's Eve party. They smiled at each other as they saw Collin's mom waiting for them on Ben's driveway. And just like at Christmas, the men of the family behaved themselves. There was so little teasing between Collin and his brother that Lauren never had a reason to retreat to the backyard. She did, however, sneak outside around 7:00pm to make a call.

"Hello, Mr. Davis. Happy New Year."

"Lauren, hello! Happy New Year to you too!" Mr. Davis practically beamed through the phone.

"I am sorry to bother you, but I just wanted to see if Theo Briggs had come by the apartment building again."

Lauren held her breath.

"Oh yes, about 5 days after I emailed you."

"What happened?"

"Not much. I saw him in the hallway so I went to talk to him. I told him to leave immediately. He laughed at me. So...," Mr. Davis paused. "I gave him your message."

"And? What was his reaction?"

Mr. Davis let out a deep belly laugh.

"I think he understood. He practically ran out the door."

Lauren and Mr. Davis chatted for a minute more and then said goodbye, wishing each other a very happy 2024.

Just as Lauren hung up, her phone pinged with an incoming email. She let out a cheer as she read the subject line.

CONGRATULATIONS! Your application is ACCEPTED

She turned around and ran into the house.

"Guess who enrolled in photography classes again?!"

The End

About the Author

Susan Ulrich Kruse is a new author. Born in Texas but raised in Iowa on a healthy dose of police dramas and true crime television, her first attempt at writing was when she bought herself a notebook and decided she was going to write a book. The book never made it past page one but her love of a good spiral notebook remains to this day!

Many years later, Susan graduated from The University of Iowa where she met her husband, and they raised two sons in the Kansas City area.

When she's not working, Susan will be on the hunt for a good British procedural or true crime documentary. She, her husband and the family dog split their time between living in Florida and Missouri.

The Stall is Susan's debut novella.

Printed in Great Britain
by Amazon

46071054R00108